H

A

DON'T CRY
FOR ME,
HOT PASTRAMI

1

I know we're in trouble when the wooden handicapped ramp leading to the side entrance of the temple disappears—replaced by a swaying gangplank. The sight of Rabbi Kevin Kapstein hardly relieves my fears—he's wearing a white yachting cap as he waves the board members off the gangplank and into a transformed Blumberg Social Hall.

It only takes two *ahoys* from Essie Sue Margolis, Kevin's mentor and my worst nightmare, to convince me I should be home watching *Law and Order* instead of *Kvetching and Chaos,* as I've come to call our monthly Board of Directors' meetings at Temple Rita. I gulp down two aspirin tablets before even taking off my jacket. This headache insurance hasn't worked yet, but by now it's a habit.

"My hearties, have I got a surprise for you!"

Ignoring the group shudder, Essie Sue, resplendent in a crisp navy blue sailor suit and hat, reaches for her third metaphor of the night, and we've only been here five minutes.

"Now, voyagers. I'm aware that you probably don't know what I'm talking about, nautically speaking. But you will."

"That's never stopped you before. Get on with the program."

Bubba Copeland has a short fuse and a long memory regarding Essie Sue and her fund-raising efforts. Essie Sue's still trying to commission a solid marble, five-thousand-pound Queen Esther statue in memory of her late sister Marla, who dropped dead on the floor of The Hot Bagel a few years ago. We're all paying for it, in more ways than one. Her latest fiasco, a nationwide sale of reduced-calorie matzo balls, almost killed me last year. Literally.

"All will be revealed, Bubba, before we adjorn to the social hall for navy bean soup in honor of our newest fund-raiser."

"With Oreos?"

That's Mr. Chernoff—not that he'll sway Essie Sue one way or another.

"Stuff it, Herman. I'm talking originality here. The

rabbi has given his blessing to this event. You're going to love it."

I'm feeling queasy already. "So is this *event* going into the minutes as a done deal, or were we called here to vote on something? You're not planning to do an end run on the temple bylaws again, are you?"

"Please, Ruby—you and your constitutional concerns. Don't you have any imagination?"

"Yeah, I'm imagining that if this project has already been blessed by you and Kevin, we don't have a chance."

"All right, then I'll do it by the book. Are you ready, Parliamentarian?"

About as ready as Rachel Gettleman will ever be, considering that her qualifications for the job were that her brother-in-law registered voters in Travis County from 1965 to 1973.

"Here's the surprise. I move that our new fund-raising project be a cruise of the Jewish Caribbean, featuring St. Thomas in the U.S. Virgin Islands. Anchors aweigh! Play the tape, Rabbi."

Before Kevin presses the button on *Naval Hymns from Down Under,* I press a point of order.

"Wait a minute—there *is* no Jewish Caribbean."

Essie Sue's ready for me.

"Of course there is. Jews sailed to the Caribbean before Poland ever knew a rabbi. I've researched this, Ruby. Don't think just because you're a rabbi's wife that you're the only Jewish historian around here."

"I'm no longer a rabbi's wife, and I don't know any

Jewish historians in Eternal. Do you?" My husband, Stu, was rabbi of the temple before he was killed a few years ago. It took all his energy to keep Essie Sue in check, but she's ruled the roost since Stu's successor, Kevin Kapstein, took over.

"Are you trying to say that Jews *lived* in the Caribbean, Essie Sue? That's a far cry from—"

"I'm not going to let you spoil my nautical evening, Ruby. There's a motion on the floor."

I can tell Bubba Copeland's catching my headache—the vein near his temple is enlarging as he speaks. "There's motion, all right. I'm getting seasick. What's the deal here? Clue us in, Essie Sue, before I move to adjourn."

"I wanted everyone to catch the spirit first, but since you're all so oppositional tonight, I'll have to change my tactics. We need to go into executive session."

Rachel Gettleman doesn't look amused.

"We've never been in executive session before. Speaking as Parliamentarian, just what does executive session mean, exactly?"

"It means we meet without the rabbi."

"That's it? Am I supposed to escort him out?"

"I'll escort him out. Sorry, Rabbi. I was driven to this by extreme lack of cooperation."

"Point of order." Kevin's fighting back. "I want to lodge a formal protest. I rented this outfit."

"No way I'm dealing with a formal protest." Rachel's out of her seat. "Point of parliamentary overload. What do I do now, Essie Sue?"

"Hold it, Rachel. Go check on the anchor carved in ice, Rabbi—this won't take long. My committee will reimburse you for the yachting suit."

"Your committee?"

Essie Sue manages to nudge Kevin out the door, squelch the last question from the assemblage, and ease Rachel back into her seat before staring down the room.

"Okay, people. This is serious."

"You're going to have a helluva time talking serious to a background of 'Anchors Aweigh.'"

"I know, Bubba, but that was merely window dressing to make the medicine go down. I'm not just fund-raising here. I'm trying to save the rabbi."

"Save him? From what?" Brother Copeland, younger brother to Bubba—same substance, different style— pipes in where Bubba can't go. Essie Sue favors Brother over Bubba, so Brother can get more out of her.

"Gather around, everybody, and don't breathe a word of this. This is board business, okay?"

"Yeah, yeah. Just tell us."

"No, Bubba. I want sworn oaths from all of you. Raise your hands."

Curiosity overcomes common sense, and we all dutifully raise our hands to swear confidentiality. Right.

"Do you all swear not to tell, not ever to tell what I'm going to tell you, so help you God?"

This is too much. "I'm not swearing to God on this, Essie Sue."

"Okay, Ruby, so we'll swear on my copy of the *Jewish*

Forward—it has a national circulation. Good enough for you?"

I refrain from raising my hand altogether, but she ignores me and pulls out a huge file folder from her briefcase at the end of the table.

"People, these are the top-secret results of a questionnaire I submitted to a temple focus group at my own expense. I made copies for everyone. Read it and weep."

"Focus group? Who do you think you are, Dick Morris?" Bubba's reaching for his copy as he speaks, of course.

"This is the way things are done in the modern world, Bubba. We're nothing if not *with it* here at Temple Rita. I regret to inform you that my survey shows our beloved rabbi's job-approval rating has fallen to an all-time low."

"What did you expect?" Brother yells. "He squeaked by the Rabbinic Selection Committee by a majority of one."

"He did not. He was voted in unanimously."

"Oh, sure, after you made the secretary erase the vote and put in *Unanimous* on pain of death."

"That was a courtesy. All organizations do it. This poll was scientifically calculated to compute the rabbi's charisma quotient. On the first question, 'Is our rabbi as dynamic as you thought he would be?' Rabbi Kapstein unfortunately scored one percent."

"This is too painful, Essie Sue. Just let us read it to ourselves."

"No pain, no gain, Ruby, but if you insist, I'll give on that point."

I don't think it can get worse, but then I read the sample questions:

Leadership Ability—If Rabbi Kapstein were to the temple as Moshe Dayan was to the Israelis, would you follow him into battle? Yes: 2 percent.

Intellectual Prowess—Do the rabbi's sermons pique your curiosity? Not really: 97 percent.

Does the rabbi stimulate our mission as a light unto the nations? Dim: 98 percent.

"Pardon my asking, but just who in the congregation did you focus on for these answers, Essie Sue?"

"They shall remain nameless, Ruby. End of story."

"So what are we supposed to do with this?"

"That's why we're here. The rabbi is obviously not putting his best foot forward."

"I'd say he was putting his foot *in* it."

"Be that as it may, Brother, the man needs help, and I, for one, feel he's misunderstood. That's why this cruise is going to be his salvation. He'll be our trip guide, showcasing his leadership abilities, and he'll educate us in the history and culture of the Jews of the Caribbean—that takes care of the intellect thing."

Essie Sue flicks a red-manicured little finger at the Parliamentarian, who reacts in Pavlovian fashion:

"There's a motion on the floor. All in favor, say *aye*."

No hands go up.

"Does anyone here want to go through the rabbinical selection process twice in three years?"

All hands are up, including, I have to say, mine.

Essie Sue, beaming, goes to the door.

"Ahoy, Rabbi—bring on the navy bean soup."

2

E-mail from: Ruby
To: Nan
Subject: *Cruisin' for a Bruisin'*

Congrats on your legal internship—even
though you probably don't need it after
working for a lawyer all those years.
But you'll get to draft your own material, yes? And become indispensable to
the firm for the future—ha. I hope they
give you the independence you want.

   Don't bite my head off, but now that
you're in the groove, schoolwise, what
about your personal life? I haven't

heard the word *date* in your vocabulary since you gave me your recipe for granola mix. Look around in class—you never can tell who might be lying in wait.

Update on Essie Sue's cruise plans: things are more relaxed since she accepted my terms for assistance—that I help make the arrangements as a non-traveling participant. I can keep my cool as long as I know I don't have to be one of her little tourists. I've done some Internet research on the cruises, but so far, she hasn't taken any of my suggestions. She must have some angle. I'm waiting for the shoe to drop.

E-mail from: Nan
To: Ruby
Subject: *Et Tu?*

Pardon me, but shouldn't *you* be making room for a personal life? Unless you count Kevin as a *date* and not just a nut—and as I assume you'd rather be dead than do that, your own granola pile looks a little sparse to me, babe. Answer. (And we're not counting your three-legged golden retriever here—Oy Vey's cute, but this is not the companion I see in your future.)

As for my not needing this legal internship, surely you're not equating my former employer, Stanford P. Jerk,

Esquire, with my *experience*, are you?
As a role model for malpractice, maybe.
I'm trying to forget everything Berke
taught me.
   Anything new from oceanside?

E-mail from: Ruby
To: Nan
Subject: *Funny You Should Ask*

This just came in the mail, on a blue
paper flyer:

   MASS MAILING TO MY CRUISE
   COMMITTEE   FROM YOUR CHAIRWOMAN

   Yo Sea-mates!
   I've just learned through the kosher
   grapevine that my long-lost cousin Harry
   Goldberg, now known as Captain Horatio
   Goldberg, is one of the few (Who knows?
   Maybe the only Jew.) to be captain of a
   bona fide cruise ship. Captain Goldberg
   is following in the footsteps of
   Christopher Columbus, who, as you know,
   was probably also Jewish.
   Captain Goldberg is currently sail-
   ing the Caribbean for Bargain Cruise
   Lines—We Pass Waters Where Others Fear
   to Tread.
   The best news is that after tough
   negotiations behind the scenes, the
   cruise line is willing to go wholesale

for fund-raising purposes, and we have
sealed a discount deal.
    This is confidential. More later.
                    Essie Sue Margolis

    So, Nan, what do you think the odds
are that she had this deal with the
cousin up her sleeve all along?
    Ho Ho Ho!

3

The Hot Bagel is the closest thing to a community center we have in our little town of Eternal, Texas (fast becoming a suburb of Austin since the freeway was expanded). I hang out here a lot since I became part-owner of the place with my friend Milt Aboud. In the nonbagel half of my life, I'm a computer consultant, which used to be a unique job in Eternal until half of Silicon Valley moved here to join Dell Computer. As long as I pay attention to both my occupations, I can get by—unless your definition of *getting by* includes a personal life.

Essie Sue's attempts to make me relive my entire adulthood as a clergy wife by becoming the Bride of

Frankenstein (excuse me, make that bride of Kapstein) continue to fail abysmally, but that doesn't stop her from trying, despite the fact that I'm not the least bit interested in Kevin. If he'd quit catering to Essie Sue, he'd know he feels the same way about me. From time to time, he deigns to look down favorably upon me from the heights of his ego, but then realizes I have a mind inside my head, not a mirror. Kevin's idea of compatibility with a woman is not the usual *I likka you, you likka me*—with him, it's more *I love me, you love me, so we'll both get along famously.*

Tonight we're being not-so-subtly matched again at Pastrami Piracy, the latest fund-raising extravaganza, where for twenty-five dollars a raffle ticket, anyone with two feet and cash can sign up to win ten whole pastramis as second prizes, or the first prize of a Caribbean cruise straight from Bargain Cruise Lines. I told Essie Sue her attempt to combine the word *Piracy* with one of her notoriously rigged raffles would be a tad too realistic, but here we are.

My business partner Milt didn't speak to me for three days when I said yes to this event, but I figured it would be good for business. So far, we've sold a lot of bagels to the hundred people who've shown up, but Milt doesn't care.

"I'd rather starve than work with that woman."

"Just think—she'll be away on the cruise and you won't have to see her." Pretty pathetic, but it's all I can think of as a comeback.

He ignores me. "She even went to San Antonio to

order those pastramis, instead of getting them through me—can you believe it?"

"You should be glad, Milt. If anything went wrong with them, she'd blame you."

"You've got a point. She told me she thought of raffling pastramis because they went with bagels, but when I pressed her, she admitted she got a deal on ten for the price of five from some connection through Mexico, so she worked them into the concept."

"Oh, great. She should have put 'win at your own risk' on the raffle tickets."

"I just want this evening over, Ruby. Whoa—I'm outa here. She's coming this way."

Milt disappears into the kitchen and I'm stuck, as usual.

"It's a fabulous evening, Ruby—even having it here at the bakery is okay." Essie Sue's glowing.

"Gee, thanks, I think."

"We've sold a bunch of raffle tickets, not including the ones we unloaded in advance. We'd have done even better if I'd had time to decorate the bakery like a cruise ship."

"You already did your decorating at the board meeting. Besides, I had a hard enough time getting Milt to have the party here—there was no way he'd agree to let you come in and tear the place apart."

"He's a boor. Thank goodness my niece Glenda didn't marry him." Milt and Essie Sue go way back, but that's another story.

"Can you get a stool for me, Ruby? I'm going to stand on one of the tables."

"Excuse me?"

"I want everyone to see me when I draw the winning tickets."

"Sit on the table, Essie Sue—they can still see you."

"Nightclub-singer style? Okay. It might look good with this slit skirt, if I position my legs right. At least I've still got my figure."

That's a dig at me, even though there aren't as many pounds between us as there are years. It's just that those pounds are all around my waistline in one bunch. In return, I get to eat like a normal person and she gets to call a lettuce leaf lunch. I decided a long time ago it was a fair trade-off.

She swivels herself up onto a table in the center of the room and crosses her legs. The shock value of her nightclub routine seems to have bypassed the crowd, but she forges ahead.

"Ladies and gentlemen, welcome to Pastrami Piracy. We're giving away ten whole pastramis and one free chance for piracy on the high seas, where Blackbeard robbed and plundered. These hot pastramis will feed seventy-five people if you slice them thin—and you should, if you don't want a coronary."

I don't know about anyone else here, but I'm thinking that this is not such a great come-on for prospective passengers. She's supposedly planning to make money from commissions on the discount cruise tickets she sells—and raffling the free trip should whet people's appetites—if the pastramis don't.

"And now for the main event." Essie Sue has even uncrossed her legs for the big announcement. "The owners of Bargain Cruise Lines have graciously donated a lovely stateroom as first prize in our raffle. And to those of you who don't win first prize, I can only say that for a few measly dollars—money you'd undoubtedly squander on dull necessities—you can accompany our lucky winner and sail in the footsteps of the pirates."

Wow, she always did have a way with words—that last should really reel 'em in.

"To conduct the ticket drawing, I'd like to introduce a distinguished surprise guest." She jumps down from her perch on the table and plunges into the crowd, emerging with a balding, bespectacled little man who's having difficulty holding on to her hand. In fact, he's being dragged at a rapid pace. Essie Sue doesn't fool around.

"People, this is history professor Willie Bob Gonzales, of Buda Community College in Buda, Texas, our official lecturer for the cruise. Professor Gonzales's specialty is 'The Jews of the Inquisition and What Happened to Them.'"

The professor looks a little uncomfortable at having his life's work summarized so brilliantly, but he's apparently already discovered, like the rest of us, that it's safer to acquiesce. He's not invited to say anything, but Essie Sue still has his hand so he can't leave.

"As you know, people, the Caribbean is full of Spanish Jews, and this trip is all going to be very intellectual. The ship also has two casinos." I guess this fact was thrown in for the benefit of the rest of us—Essie Sue is not dumb when it comes to soliciting funds—but the information does not appear to have surprised Professor Gonzales. He tries to shake loose, but she's stronger than he is.

"My cousins, the Bitman twins of Buda, have known Willie Bob Gonzales since he came to the college several years ago, and they recommend him highly. And they'll be sailing with us—right, Professor?"

The Bitman twins undoubtedly carry the same genes as their cousin—at least enough to make Willie Bob go pale at the mention of their names. He nods and tries for a smile at the crowd.

"So we already have myself and my husband, Hal, Professor Gonzales, my twin cousins, our spiritual leader— Rabbi Kapstein—and the winner of our raffle, who will be on our way to the high seas. I'm sure the rest of you will join our ranks soon. I certainly expect all the pastrami winners to fork up fares for the voyage—it's only fair."

With that sort of encouragement, you'd think this crowd would be heading for the exits, but they're all gathered around, tickets in hand, for the big drawing.

Professor Gonzales sticks his hand ten times into the empty five-gallon ice cream carton Essie Sue has decorated as a rum barrel. Ten lucky winners come up to receive certificates for their pastramis. I know it's only coincidence that all of them are either related to Essie Sue or are members of the fund-raising committee. Not that she rewards her own—before the lucky winners receive their certificates, they're required to sign up for the Temple Rita cruise. The actual pastramis will come whenever the shipment can get through Customs, I presume. If the recipients are lucky, maybe the pastramis'll be delivered while they're away in the Caribbean—then they won't have to eat them.

"And now for the pièce de résistance. I shall ask Professor Gonzales to step down and call forward our own Rabbi Kevin Kapstein to draw the grand prize winner."

Kevin, in a black pinstriped suit, vest, and power-red tie, formally shakes Essie Sue's hand, waves to the crowd, and, with an obviously well-rehearsed gesture, plunges his hand into the ice cream carton and hands the winning ticket unread to Essie Sue.

I should have seen it coming from the big smirk on Kevin's face before Essie Sue even looked at the paper.

Essie Sue holds the ticket aloft. "The winner is—our late lamented rabbi's wife, Ruby Rothman. Ruby, come on down!"

Late lamented is right. Or *demented* not to have shouted the crowd down then and there. There were so many cheers and whoops from Essie Sue's minions, followed by the fastest adjournment on record, that by the time I had a chance to say something, there was no one to say it to except Milt and the cleanup crew. Essie Sue pulled a deliberate disappearing act, and I know she did it to avoid hearing any protests from my end—her usual MO at parties she gives is to meet and greet until the last guest gasps.

"Now I've got to go to all the trouble to get out of this."

"Gracefully?" Milt's pouring me some extra-hot coffee the way I like it, black. We're curled up in two of the easy chairs I moved into The Hot Bagel when I became part-owner and decided to make the place less cavernous and more homey.

"Who says *gracefully*? I just want out. When Essie Sue first asked me to help, I told her I'd work behind the scenes as long as I didn't have to go on the cruise."

"So why do you think she wants you there?" He's pushing a warm pumpernickel bagel my way.

"Probably because she doesn't want to depend on Kevin to keep things together."

"Or maybe this is her way of driving the two of *you* together."

"She can do that at home." I'm just biting into the chewy bagel when something nags at my brain: "Hey, what's missing here, Miltie? Where's all the hostility this woman usually brings out in you? And why are you being so sanguine?"

"I'm *that* transparent?"

"Ha—if you're so shocked, ask your wife. Grace says around the house she can see through you like a sieve."

"I really need my wife and my business partner ganging up on me."

"We haven't, so far. Besides, I'm just interested in the here and now, and you're *way* too tame."

"Well, I was just thinking that you've had a tight year financially, and this *is* a free trip, no matter what the motivation. Maybe once you're in the islands, you could get away from the Temple Rita gang during the day trips and just chill out by that emerald-green water. Could be you need it."

"I appreciate the sentiment, but you know how hard it is to shake these people. I'd come back more stressed than ever."

"You could tell her you'll only accept the prize if she considers you a guest—a total tourist, and not part of the leadership. That way, you'd be free to come and go. You could discover the beaches where the locals hang out."

"Sounds great, if I were down there by myself." I'm on my second cup of coffee—caffeine doesn't bother me, night or day.

"Don't be so stubborn, Ruby—you can't afford to *go* down there by yourself. And pardon me for being blunt, but don't you realize how damn edgy you've been lately?"

"Aha—now you're sending me a message."

"Since you don't listen to me nice, then listen to me nasty, okay? You need the rest after juggling two jobs all year. Finesse these people and find a way to have a good time on your own. What's so bad about a Caribbean cruise, anyway?"

For not anticipating the answer to that little question, Milt is going to owe me big.

5

I should have known our lives were expendable at two this afternoon when I first saw the embarkation building of Bargain Cruise Lines—a gigantic prefabricated warehouse perched on the waters of Galveston Bay. Its purpose is obviously to facilitate moving cargo— namely, us—from shore to ship as fast as humanly possible. Or inhumanly, as is proving to be the case two hours later.

There are thousands of people here—not hundreds, as I had always imagined. I'm thinking *QE2*—suave, white- jacketed stewards chattily escorting us to our cabins. What I'm getting is *Y3K*—it's going to take at least a century to be cattle-prodded through this maze, and there's not a steward in sight.

The only saving grace is that our star lecturer, Professor Willie Bob Gonzales, must have had time by now to sober up. The professor celebrated early upon our arrival at the George Bush International Airport en route to the Port of Galveston—he chugalugged half a bottle of Essie Sue's champagne surprise and used the other half to christen the American Airlines counter. Fortunately, the bottle didn't break and Essie Sue convinced the airline personnel it was all a huge mistake. How she intimidated them, I have no idea—although I did hear the words *governor* and *senator* thrown around.

"I think the poor man is nervous about the trip," is all Essie Sue could summon up in explanation. That's obvious—Willie Bob was skittish at the raffle drawing, too— but who wouldn't be after she dragged him up to the microphone and wouldn't let go? Apparently, he often lectures on shipboard, but even an idiot would realize that a cruise with Essie Sue is not your usual cup o' brine, and this man is no idiot. He's now jostling for position with the other twenty-five of us lucky members of the Temple Rita contingent as we form an unruly line and prepare to board ship. The ship is nowhere in sight, by the way—this embarkation palace is hooked up to the bowels of the *Bargain II* in such a Byzantine manner that we could just as well be surging headlong into the amazon.com warehouse in Seattle. But hey, at least I'm not paying for this.

So far, all I've seen of water is the lukewarm fountain

where I waited fifteen minutes to sip—which is quite a feat while balancing three carry-on bags. There are lines for everything—driver's license, birth certificate, for those with passports, and a line for people who think they're in the wrong line—culminating in a series of folding tables staffed, if one can use that word, by people drinking Cokes and yawning. I wish I had one of the Cokes.

As if this relaxing start to our cruise needed any improvement, Kevin, in a sweat, is breathing down my neck and whining.

"This stuff is too heavy, Ruby. Can you help me?"

"No."

"Essie Sue made me carry Professor Gonzales's backpack when he started weaving around. I think you should take a turn."

"No."

"She told me to meet them at this line to have our picture taken, and I've already been here twenty minutes."

"Is that what we're in line for, Kevin? I can't even see the end of it. I'm skipping this—I have my own camera."

"No, it's an official photo. You have to have it taken—they won't let you on the boat unless you do."

"I think it's *ship,* not *boat.* And I'm pretty sure it's optional. This is one of those commercial deals where they pose you in front of a backdrop that says *Welcome* or something." I step out of line and look. He's right—you have to go through the photo setup to get to the wide corridor leading to the ship. There's no backdrop here, though—the cruise line has cut a few corners, assigning a guy to stand with a limp *Bargain II* flag in back of the posed passengers. A harbinger of things to come, I suspect.

Kevin knocks into me. "Where's Essie Sue? I'm supposed to be saving her a place in line."

"Forget saving her anything, unless you want to be mobbed by frustrated travelers."

Right on cue, Essie Sue pushes her way in from the side, ignoring all protesters. With one arm firmly around Willie Bob Gonzales and the other holding a huge ice chest, she hits from the rear and tries to foist the ice chest on me.

"Hold it, Essie Sue. Where's your better half? Can't he help you?"

"No, I told Hal to bring up the rear. I don't want our group getting separated."

"It's too late now—I don't see any of them. Relax and get your picture taken."

I realize I've said the wrong thing—to this woman, a photo without primping is off the radar.

"I look horrible. Hold Professor Gonzales, Ruby, while I find my lipstick."

Before I can run, she drapes Willie Bob's arm around my neck and lets go. His glasses are half off, and the sailor hat she's bought him is cocked on the side of his head. As if I'm not in enough trouble, the passengers she's cut in front of are milling around us—not a pretty sight.

"Keep him," she yells. "I want to have my picture taken with the rabbi. You can have the professor."

"You're next." The photographer almost dares me not

to have my picture taken—the stress of photographing two thousand people might have gotten to him. Before I know it, I'm posing with Willie Bob Gonzales draped around me. He has yet to say a word.

The flash goes off and Willie Bob goes down.

"Passed out," Essie Sue wails. "I've had it with him."

Stepping over the professor, she drags Kevin in front of the photographer, straightens Kevin's jacket collar, and glares at him.

"Rabbi, say *cheese.*"

Not only does Kevin say *cheese,* he joins Essie Sue in a wide grin—never say that these two lack compassion. Having completed the photo op, they stare at me as I attempt to raise the dead.

Willie Bob has gone under in a big way. He's on his back, lying over my shoes so that I can't stoop down without fear of landing on him. Talk about feeling off balance—I was already disoriented in the midst of this cast of thousands, and now I'm looking down at the face of a passed-out drunk. To make things worse, people are literally stepping over us to have their pictures taken and board the ship.

I do a choke hold on Essie Sue, using the sleeves of the nautical sweater she's casually thrown over her shoulders.

"Listen, Essie Sue—we're in trouble here. Get me help fast before the crowd tramples on the professor. And don't tell me we can drag him onto the ship."

I guess I got through to her—she orders Kevin to go find someone official. He comes back with the Bitman twins from Buda, Essie Sue's cousins, who've shown up in line. At least they are two live bodies who know this man well.

"Should I get a doctor," one twin says, "or is this just from too much champagne? He was having a pretty good time at the airport."

I look at the other twin, who actually seems sentient.

"He needs help," she says.

After minutes that seem like hours, the ship's doctor finally appears, thanks to the second twin. He lifts Willie Bob off my feet, which are as numb as I am, kneels to do a quick exam, and then looks up.

"Is he just dead drunk?" Essie Sue asks the doctor.

"He's just dead."

6

At eight o'clock, only two hours after the scheduled sailing time, a few of us are huddled around a table on the ship's top deck as it pulls out from port. We can't see much—the wind is up and a fog has rolled in. I have yet to view that azure-blue Caribbean I've been waiting for—maybe tomorrow. A waiter is hawking a tray full of frozen daiquiris—looking more like strawberry sundaes than anything alcoholic—at distinctly nonbargain prices, but none of us is in the mood to imbibe. The police have questioned us as part of a fairly routine inquiry, and Professor Gonzales's body, accompanied by the Bitman twins, will soon be headed back to his family in Buda.

The doctor was right. Despite his attempts to revive Willie Bob—first by mouth and then by equipment brought from the ship's hospital—the professor was dead. There were no apparent signs of trauma, unless you counted my trauma—I was in shock. I told the doctor that he had swayed and his breath had smelled of alcohol, but he didn't hit himself on the head when he fell. The general consensus, concurred with by all the subsequent medical personnel, was that Willie Bob had died of a heart attack aggravated by the excitement and the champagne.

"This isn't fair." Kevin's wailing again.

"Sudden death certainly isn't fair, Kevin," I say. I'm feeling that as clergy he should be comforting us, not the other way around, but then, I'm used to him.

"It's not fair that I now have to be the teacher on the trip. Essie Sue says I have to take Professor Gonzales's place. I was just supposed to be the leader, not the teacher."

"Take advantage of the opportunity to educate us, Rabbi," Essie Sue says. "You've got all his notes—it should be easy. Remember what I told you—this is your chance to shine. Let's toast to the professor and dedicate our search for knowledge to him. He would have wanted us to continue our cruise."

She summons the waiter to serve the alcoholic confections, and calls for drinks all around. I can't take this—not after the day we've gone through. And the professor's not cold in his grave yet. I'm getting up to go back to my cabin, when I hear a piercing alarm from the public address system, and a voice that I'd know anywhere was related to Essie Sue.

"Passengers, this is your captain speaking."

"Listen to that Continental accent. Isn't it thrilling?"

"Hush, Essie Sue—I want to hear what he's saying."

What he's saying is that we're having an emergency drill. We all have to go down six floors to our cabins to put on orange life preservers, and then come up six floors to stand by our lifeboats. Our group, the super-bargain party, is quartered on the lowest deck, of course—the one that the ship's stabilizer doesn't quite stabilize.

"Is he kidding?" Kevin says. "And why is the waiter putting our drinks back on the tray?"

"A drill is routine at the beginning of a cruise," I tell him. "The waiter can't serve now."

"Forget it," Essie Sue says. She starts grabbing drinks back off the tray. "Captain Horatio Goldberg is my cousin," she tells the waiter. "I'm sure he has complete confidence in us to do the right thing in a crisis. We're staying here."

"Well, I'm not," I say as I head for the stairs. I have a big stake in finding out what to do if the *Bargain II* sinks, especially since I noticed the handle of the porthole in my cabin is held together by something that looks suspiciously like bubble gum.

I'm already late—one of the bottom floors of this place, or *lower deck* as we say in ship-speak, is deserted as I race into my cabin to find the life preserver that's supposed to be in plain view. It isn't. I finally locate the big orange vest under the bunk bed, but don't have time to do anything about the dangling white straps hanging out in every direction. Now I have that added weight as I climb the six flights of stairs to report to our captain. What a glorious vacation so far—and this is only the first day.

I finally glimpse another human being on the stair above me as I make my final ascent to the main deck—or rather, I see his rear end. And an awfully cute one, I might add, clad in faded jeans going full length down long legs to barefoot sandals. There's a white tee shirt on his well-sculpted top half, underlying a perfectly put together orange life jacket.

"Wait up," I say, but he doesn't hear me—probably because there's no air left to go through my vocal cords—it's all been used to propel me up five flights of stairs so far. Not only does he not hear me, he's also letting the heavy door to the main deck slam in my face. I'm almost pushed backward, but I force the door open and follow Mr. Sweetcheeks. It occurs to me that if this were a real drill, the ship would have sunk by now and we'd both be sleeping with the fishes in the stairwell.

"Hey, wait up," I try again. "Can you tell me where we're supposed to be?"

"The sign says down this corridor and out the door to the deck."

He looks me up and down and opens the door, seeming totally uncurious about where I've emerged from. I'm no doubt a ravishing sight in a pool of sweat with six white straps flapping from my life jacket.

So this is where everybody went. Hundreds of people are lined up for the lifeboat drill on this particular deck, and they all seem to be staring at us. Our deck steward runs over and tries to take each of us by the hand, kindergarten style.

"You're not supposed to be late—this is very important."

Neither of us is making it easy for him—we've independently jerked our hands away.

"Well, at least get in line."

We both step in line, but I'm immediately yanked out again by another steward.

"Look at her loose life jacket. She's flapping."

My late-mate rolls his eyes, and everyone else is smirking, but I'm shameless.

"Can I copy yours?" I ask him. I start copying, but it's not helping—my fingers don't work when I'm in a hurry.

"I'll strap the back ones for no charge."

Before my partner can display his great generosity, a siren wails and the steward wags his finger at us.

"It's all over, so don't bother."

A whole deckful of people starts milling around us on their way to the stairs. They're also filling the elevators, which had been shut down during the drill.

"It ought to take about an hour to get down to the lower deck where the engine fumes are," Mr. Sweetcheeks says. "Wanna go check out the lifeboats we missed inspecting?"

"Yeah, it shouldn't be a total waste, and I don't trust this ship, anyway."

As we head toward the lifeboats, he turns and sticks out his hand.

"I'm Ed Levinger."

I decide not to tell him I've already named him. He doesn't look like the cruise type to me. But then, neither do I, I hope.

"I'm Ruby Rothman. I guess we're both stuck down on the cheapie deck."

"I'm two decks up from the bottom," he says, "but it's a freebie. I'm doing a travel piece."

"I won a raffle, so we're even." A raffle sounds a lot dorkier than a travel piece, so obviously, we're *not* even, but I tried.

"Are you with a group?"

"Oh yes—you can't miss us." Wait till he gets a load of our fearless leader, Essie Sue. I think I'll introduce him to the whole gang as soon as possible, and see how he holds up. By my calculations, they should now be at the bottom of the sea on the sunken ship, sharing strawberry daiquiries with the sharks.

7

"See—I told you it was wasted effort to go to the fire drill."

Essie Sue has made her way to the outdoor deck. How lucky for me.

"So why are you here?" I ask her.

"The elevators are working now, so I thought I'd see what all the fuss was about. What did we miss?"

"Just the drill."

"Did they take names?"

"I have no idea."

"The captain can take care of it for me. I have friends in high places," she adds for Mr. Sweetcheeks's benefit. "And you are . . . ?"

"Ed Levinger."

"From?"

"San Antonio."

If he thinks *he's* conducting the interviews from now on, he's in for a shock. I realize, though, that if I just keep quiet for five minutes, I'll know all about this guy without having to open my mouth.

Ed folds his legs and sits down on the deck floor—he must have a hunch this will last awhile. Or else, he hopes he'll get rid of her—I don't think she'll risk her white pants on the deck.

"I'm with Ruby," she says by way of introduction. Ed cocks his head, shoves a stray lock of brown hair from his forehead, and looks at me for confirmation.

"Sort of," I say. "She's part of our group."

"More than a part," she says. "I organized the whole trip." She sits down on the edge of a chaise longue so she's perched a few inches above him—her favorite angle. This leaves me standing here looking down at both of them. I'd like to take this opportunity to scoot, but I'm afraid to leave them alone without being here to defend myself.

"Did you know Ruby was a rabbi's wife?"

Well, that was fast. And I thought I was going to learn something about *him*.

"Mr. Levinger and I just came up the stairs together, Essie Sue. We've barely exchanged names, much less life histories." I want to say I haven't been anybody's wife for a while now, but I don't want her defining my conversations.

The door to the deck opens and Kevin comes over, panting. A diversion—I've never been so glad to see him.

"I've been looking for you on every deck, Ruby. Those stairs are killers."

"Didn't you know the elevators were working again?" Essie Sue says.

"*Now* you tell me. Listen, Ruby, you have to come to my cabin and meet with me. I'm supposed to give my first class in Caribbean Jewish history tomorrow morning, and I'm not ready."

"I told you—you'll do fine," Essie Sue says. "Meet Ruby's friend from San Antonio. This is our spiritual leader, Rabbi Kapstein."

Kevin hikes up his plaid walking shorts with one hand and sticks out the other. The good news is he's shed his black wing tips and socks. The bad news is he's replaced them with leather house slippers. Nevertheless, he seems pleased with the introduction as a spiritual leader. Ed stands up to shake hands.

"Just tending my flock," Kevin says to Ed, who politely nods his head as Essie Sue beams. This man certainly is unflappable—maybe it's the journalistic training. I notice he's also inclined to listen more than to talk—he's contributed all of three words to the conversation.

Maybe I could take lessons.

"Listen, Ruby, this is important. You've got to come with me right now, so I can try out the outline I found in the backpack. Maybe you can help me figure out what's supposed to go between the lines."

"Kevin, I'm tired—give me a chance to get my bearings."

"One hour, Ruby. Only one hour to start me out and I promise I'll work on this all night by myself."

"Okay, I'll start you off, Kevin, but that's it."

Essie Sue reaches up and pats my leg—I'm still standing stupidly on the deck waiting for all this to go away.

"That's the least you could do, Ruby—after all, you are getting this trip at no charge."

By this point, I'm glancing sideways at blasé Ed Levinger, wondering how he can keep from reacting. My life's an open book, so what else is new? And to make things worse, Kevin's still not placated.

"Why did this have to happen, Ruby? Why did Professor Gonzales have to die before he gave his lectures?"

Suddenly, Ed's not blasé anymore. "Did you say Professor Gonzales was dead?"

"You're pale, Ed," I say. "Maybe you'd better sit down again."

This time, he flops down on one of the chairs pulled up to a table near Essie Sue's chaise. I take the other chair at the table, and Kevin's left standing, still staring at Ed. He's keeping his distance, and I can't say I blame him.

"Did you know Professor Gonzales?" I ask.

"Yes," he says. "Well, more yes than no, I guess. I met him on one other trip to the islands, and I knew he lectured on these ships occasionally. I wasn't expecting to see him this time, but in answer to your question, I did know him."

He's looking as if he'd rather be anywhere but here at the moment.

"Maybe this wasn't the Gonzales you knew," Essie Sue says. "It's a common name." She's giving him the once-over, obviously picking up on his discomfort.

"He's a professor, Essie Sue, and he made these sailings," I say, trying to head off a full-scale intrusiveness attack. "How many professors could there be?"

"How did you people know him?" Ed's making a recovery, or at least trying to, but by the time Essie Sue gives him the whole megillah about the Bitman twins and Buda Community College, he seems to fade.

"So what do you do," she says, "besides cruise?"

I'm driven to jump in again, but I guess I don't need to protect someone I hardly know.

"I'm a journalist."

"A travel writer?" she asks.

"Sometimes. On this trip."

He eases himself up from the chair, like somebody who thinks he's going to make a clean getaway. Think on.

"Do you work for a newspaper? Can you give the temple some publicity?"

"I'm doing a freelance article," he says, finally seeming to realize who he's dealing with, and wisely choosing not to. "Gotta go now."

"Wait," Kevin says. "If you're a journalist, could you look at my first lecture after I type it up on the professor's laptop?"

Ed sits back down. "Okay."

Now I'm shocked. But hey, it's Ed's problem now.

"This is great," Kevin says. "I'll bring it to your cabin tonight after Ruby helps me."

"You don't need both of us," I say. I'm going to be exhausted after this day, and I'd love to get out of this altogether. But there's a question nagging at me about the laptop. Before we heard the drill siren, Essie Sue said something I didn't pay attention to at the time about Kevin's having the professor's notes. I guess they're in the laptop.

"Why do you have the laptop, Kevin?"

"I made him carry it when Professor Gonzales was weaving around," Essie Sue says. "I was afraid Willie Bob would drop it in that big crowd."

"Shouldn't the laptop have gone back to his family with the body?"

"I didn't remember it at the time, Ruby," Kevin said. "When I did, I wanted to keep it until we got back and then turn it in. I know Willie Bob would want me to do a good job taking his place."

"Of course, he would," Essie Sue says. "You can follow in his footsteps as a scholar."

Dream on. Meanwhile, though, I guess Kevin's lucky to have those notes.

"Why don't you help him, Ruby?" Ed says. "I'm Jewish, but no scholar. I'll look at it after it's finished."

Sure. Now he's having second thoughts.

"I'm no maven, either, Ed."

"You'll both look at the lecture—it's settled." Essie Sue's not letting go of a good thing.

I guess I can't get out of this. "It looks as though we're all going to be busy tonight. Make it early, Kevin."

"I'll come to your cabin by ten, Ruby, and to yours by eleven, Ed. Okay?"

Ed's out of his seat already. "Yeah, sure. Eleven's fine. I'm a night owl," he says on his way out the deck door.

Kevin seems relieved, Essie Sue's looking smug about snagging another recruit, and I'm puzzled.

Just a few minutes ago Ed, who struck me as the prince of detachment, was ready to abandon our motley crew. What changed his mind?

8

Kevin's at my cabin door before I can even write a post-card home. I look at my watch and realize it's ten o'clock already, and all I've had to eat is a granola bar and some corn chips that were being served with the ill-fated daiquiris. We boarded before dinnertime with no meal scheduled for the first night—probably a cost-cutting measure. There seem to be lots of those around. Not that we'd have noticed food since our guest lecturer was dropping dead, but still. When I tried to order a snack brought to the cabin just now, I was told the kitchen had been closed down. As far as I can tell, it had never opened.

"Come on in, Kevin."

"Ruby, I'm going to have to write everything out—I can't wing this like I do my sermons."

Oh, yeah. I've noticed how he wings his sermons—soaring eagles they're not.

"Don't get so nervous about it—you're talking to the same people you preach to on Friday nights. And half of them will be hitting the slots or taking dance lessons."

"I looked at the program, Ruby. They're not giving dance lessons—it's a cost-cutting measure. I'm all there is."

Oy. This is worse than I thought. I'm trying not to think about my first night at sea sitting on my bunk squeezed in beside Kevin   we can hardly turn around. I need to get this over with.

"Okay, let's look at the laptop."

Not bad. Professor Willie Bob had a Thinkpad, and a fancy one at that. Thank goodness it's not secured—I can get in without a password.

"This is full of stuff, Kevin. The man's got his whole life in here—we have to keep this for his family."

"Yeah, after. I have to have five lectures out of this." Obviously, sympathy's taking a backseat right now.

"Well, I'm only helping you with this first one. Then you can use it as an example for the others."

There's a whole string of files on the Conversos, also known as Crypto Jews, descended from Spanish and Portuguese Jews who were forced to convert to Christianity during the Spanish and Mexican Inquisitions. According to the professor's files, thousands of Conversos now live in the American Southwest, and some are beginning to learn about their Jewish lineage for the first time.

This was Willie Bob's historical specialty.

"Ruby, the Bitman twins told me the professor was rumored to *be* a Converso, or at least people in his family were. They said that was why he was so interested."

I hadn't heard that—it *is* interesting. I'm just sorry I didn't get to know him on the cruise. Ed Levinger said he had met him on one other trip, but they didn't sound all that well acquainted.

"I'll take all these Converso files and put them together in one separate folder for you, Kevin. I'm sure they must have a printer on the ship somewhere, and we can print out the file for you in hard copy."

"What's hard copy? I want *easy*, Ruby, not hard. I thought I told you that."

"Hard copy means paper."

"Paper's good."

It's a measure of how numbed out I am that this conversation doesn't send me through the porthole. I scroll through the files and realize there's plenty of material here. I'm sure we're invading privacy, but it's just Kevin and probably five people who don't have anything else to do, so I can't worry about legalities. I'll make sure Kevin attributes everything to Professor Gonzales at the beginning of his talk.

There's one file here I'd love to take a longer look at— it's titled "Modern Conversos—Tell Family?" I'm flagging it to print out when I print Kevin's copies. I can't resist a good puzzle, and I can see all sorts of possibilities in that title.

"Let's go up to the business office, Kevin, and see if they can print out this disk for us."

"When are you going to write my speech?"

"I never said I'd write your speech. If you can get Ed to do it, fine. What I'm doing is supplying you with all the material you'll ever need for five lectures. Then it's up to you."

"Do you think Ed would write my first talk?"

"No, but he doesn't need to. Trust me, any idiot could read portions of these files and have an interesting lecture. Some rural families in the Southwest never heard of Jewish practice, yet their family rituals even include Friday-night candle-lighting. The candles are placed inside jars in an interior room of the house not visible from the windows. Some families don't eat pork or shellfish, and they bake *pan de Semita*—Semitic bread—in the spring."

"Wow, that is strange. I'm asking Ed to help anyway. He can use the selections we print out."

We take the elevator up to the business office, even though I know it's going to be closed for the night—or ought to be. But I figure this is a good way to get Kevin out of my cabin, and there's always the chance a ship's business hours are different.

We're in luck—there's a lone staffer wearing ship's whites sitting at a desk. His name tag says *Don*.

"You two want seasick medicine? They're giving it away in the lobby."

I hadn't even realized we were out on open water— so much for my whole body relaxing on this fabulous cruise.

"We just want to use this disk with your printer," I say, emphasizing that we waited until the ship's business had been taken care of to make our request. Might as well use all my advantages.

"The printer's all hooked up to another computer," Don says to me. "Give me the disk and I'll print it from here. You can keep the laptop with you."

I don't know what compels me, but I suddenly realize I haven't been alone with this laptop ever, and now it's in my hands. "Kevin, I'll be back in a few minutes. Stay and get the papers, will you? I need to do some backup, and I'll meet you here when I'm finished."

I hurry back to the cabin, lock the door in case Kevin barges in for some reason, and get out the two-port zip disk drive I've brought along with my mini-sized Toshiba computer to store images from my new digital camera. In minutes, using the fast USB port, I've backed up the professor's entire Thinkpad—it's stuffed with files, but they're all simple word-processed documents from his lecture and manuscript notes.

I make a mental note of the file names and what I might want to read later from my Toshiba screen. I have the same word-processing program Willie Bob used. Since Kevin will probably have half the ship helping him with these lectures, I won't have to worry now about who has the laptop when I need it.

I'm soon back at the business office, just in time to see Kevin emerging with a stack of nicely printed sheets. I leave most of them with him and take my copy of the "Modern Conversos—Tell Family?" file for easy bedtime reading.

9

We're dressed to kill for the captain's cocktail party. For me, that means silk pants and top with my good jewelry—in Essie Sue's case, it means serious sequins. Her white ball gown is a bit much in my opinion, but she didn't ask and I didn't tell. I do notice that, as the captain's cousin, she's appointed herself hostess for the night—she's definitely dressed for the part. Introductions have been made, and our contingent from Eternal, Texas, is now all too well known to the captain and his senior staff. The captain has put himself on a first-name basis with me, and he's leaning in way past my comfort zone.

"What do you think of the ship's orchestra, Ruby? And our newly redecorated ballroom?"

I guess this isn't the time to say the room reminds me of Las Vegas on acid, so I go into tactful, clergy-wife mode.

"Very, uh—colorful. Interesting pinks." It's *all* pink. The plush sofas surrounding the room are the same peptic pink as the bridesmaid dress I was forced to wear at Kevin's matrimonial fiasco last year. The walls are salmon pink, the chandeliers are tinted pink glass, and the floor is fuchsia tile—how they did *that* I can't imagine. The walls are mirrored reflections of pink-world. I feel like a fly trapped in cotton candy.

Captain Goldberg dyes what's left of his hair blond. It's clear he intends to cut a dashing figure in his crisp formal whites, but a few too many midnight buffets have spoiled that military splendor. And the man has bad breath. Other than that, though, he is, as Kevin says, "boss of the ship," and I'm sure he'll make the ideal date for someone. Just not me. I don't know what Essie Sue has told him about me, but if it concerns my intentions, he's misinformed.

"I want you to see the captain's quarters after the party," he says. "If you love this decor, wait until you see my more masculine lair."

"Oh, I'm sure we'll run into each other at some point," I say—"It's a long voyage." And getting longer, I might add. If the same imaginative flair extends to the captain's quarters, the lair must be boy blue. Let's hope I never find out.

The captain is undaunted. "You don't understand, my

dear. I can get you anything your heart might desire—this ship is under my complete command."

It's obvious he considers this the perfect come-on. I wonder how many conquests it's brought him—precious few, I'd imagine, unless my view of womankind is totally off base.

I'm edging away from the captain when I feel five long fingernails tapping across my shoulder blade. Talk about creepy.

"Look who's getting acquainted—I knew you two would get along famously, Horatio."

"Your friend Ruby is as charming as you described her, Essie Sue. A bit reticent, though."

Call that battle-ready. I've met his type before, and all the starched uniforms in the yacht club catalog can't make a winner out of this loser.

"Ruby, shy? Not a chance. I think she must just be toying with you—she knows how to pique your interest."

I don't know whether I'm being cast as Madame Butterfly or Carmen, but it's time to stop the music.

"Gotta go—that spinach dip is calling."

"Not yet," he says. "I want you two to meet someone important. A banker from El Paso has booked passage for this sailing. The ship's owners might be able to interest him in a partnership. He's the sophisticated type—help me impress him."

Us impress him? If he's got a brain in his head, he'll run for the hills when he notices the patches all over this barge. Gold paint can't cover up everything.

"Meet Mr. and Mrs. Marquez, Essie Sue and Ruby. I know you'll have lots in common."

"We're Sara and Jack."

A nice-looking couple—too nice for this cruise. I notice the wife got no billing at all during the captain's introductions. Figures. Late fifties, I'd guess, their hair turning silver in the same places. I'll bet it's a long-term marriage—they say couples married for a long time begin to look like each other.

"Have you met our rabbi?" Essie Sue asks. "He's giving some fascinating lectures on the A Deck this week. He needs all the support he can get."

That last is punctuated with a glare at me for sleeping late and not showing up at Kevin's lecture this morning.

"Maybe he knows the rabbi in El Paso," Sara says. "He participated in a community welcome when our bishop visited last month."

"I'm sure he does," Essie Sue says.

I'm sure he doesn't. Kevin only knows the people he has to know, and definitely avoids the competition.

Silence reigns while we all try to decide what we might have in common. Then Jack and Sara accomplish what I've been unable to do—they fade away with a minimum of fuss.

"Don't forget to drop in on the rabbi's lecture tomorrow," Essie Sue calls as they slip out of our orbit.

Encouraged by the Marquezes' exit, I decide my time has come.

I'm good at making quick getaways, but tonight I'm

outmaneuvered. With one hand, the captain waves the orchestra to break into the "Tennessee Waltz," and with the other he grabs me around the waist. I immediately go into armadillo mode.

"Everyone's looking at us," the captain says. "Can't you meld into me a little?"

In his dreams. I'm pretending I'm encased in cement from my ankles to my neck.

"Don't you dance?"

"No. I never learned."

"I heard that, Ruby." Essie Sue circles us with both arms. While she's saying "Ruby's a marvelous dancer, Horatio," I take the arm she's wrapped around me, transfer it to the captain's midsection, and leave the happy couple to waltz all over Tennessee while I head for the hors d'oeuvres.

"Quite a maneuver. I saw you wrestling with our esteemed captain."

Uh-oh. Glad I wasn't caught five seconds later by the person I'd least like to run into with a mouthful. Ed Levinger, all cleaned up in a light linen jacket and soft white shirt with open collar, has his arms held out. If I weren't so rusty it might dawn on me that this is an invitation to dance.

10

I think my sense of smell must have gone into remission for the last few years along with everything else. My new dance partner has a wonderful scent . . . a combination of just-out-of-the-shower and his own personal freshness. Whatever it is, I'm not complaining. Plus, he's a very smooth dancer. He hasn't said anything for the last five minutes, and I'm torn between not wanting to spoil the mood and my curiosity over his helping Kevin with his lecture last night.

I go for not spoiling the mood, and since the "Tennessee Waltz" performed live has been supplanted by a tape of "Close to You" while the band is on break, even the music is bearable. Ed's about five foot ten—my husband, Stu, was a lot taller, and I have to admit that medium-size is a much better fit for dancing. "Close" has an entirely different meaning when the other party's not crouching down.

Well, that's a surprise—this is probably the first comparison to Stu I've made in years that hasn't been unfavorable to the other person. Almost as good as getting rid of the comparisons altogether, but hey, nobody's perfect. Although if these green eyes gaze at me one more time, I'm liable to give up the ghost once and for all. My mind feels jet-lagged even though it shouldn't be, but my body's definitely ahead a couple of time zones.

"Mind if I cut in?" Man's voice.

"Captain's privilege!" Woman's voice.

It takes me a while to focus, but Essie Sue and her cousin Horatio seem to be trying to dance with me. No, it's just the captain, with Essie Sue pushing him forward.

"Don't forget you promised to see the captain's quarters." This man's grip is impossible to break, so I kick him. Discreetly. I'm not ready for Ed to see the real me yet.

The kick is still effective, though it's not my best shot. Horatio stumbles backward into Essie Sue, who not only breaks his fall but splits a red fingernail in the process. There is divine retribution, after all. She'd be happier if she'd fractured a hip.

"Don't you know there's no manicurist on this ship, Ruby? It's a cost-saving measure. Just a beautician, and she says she's not licensed to do hands."

"Is she licensed to kill?"

I tune out Essie Sue's answer, but it's only when Horatio tries unsuccessfully to slide his arm around my waist that I notice Ed's nowhere to be seen. Rescuing me from the captain twice in one night must not be on his agenda.

Horatio once again waves his hand and my stomach knots—whenever he waves that hand, something bad seems to happen. This time, a waiter bangs a big gong.

"A surprise, Ruby," Essie Sue says, "though you don't deserve it. Our entire party is invited to have dinner at the captain's table."

Ed left of his own free will, and I can't say I blame him. I decide I'm better off not running after him. Maybe later.

"Will you sit with me at dinner, Ruby? Essie Sue ignores me when her cousin's around." Kevin's appeared for the first time tonight—I wonder why he wasn't diving after the appetizers with the rest of us.

Better Kevin than the captain.

"What's up, Kevin? Where were you earlier?"

"I took a nap. Ed and I stayed up past midnight last night working on my lecture, and I was very stressed out teaching that class this morning. You weren't there to support me, either."

"Was Ed there?"

"No, but I did expect you."

"I was up late, too, Kevin, and I slept in. Sorry."

"Hurry up, Ruby—they're all rushing to the tables— we might miss something."

Miss something? I don't think so.

Bargain Cruise Line's Gala Dinner is a knockoff of the first order. The gleaming white linen tablecloths have never seen a cotton fiber—they're plastic. I should say *plastique*—the ship's vocabulary is rather heavy on *ques*. Likewise, the centerpieces will never see a bumblebee, unless it's painted on. Cost-cutting measures.

As for those great seafaring meals the brochures touted—make that fast-frozen chicken breasts even a self-respecting political dinner would hesitate to claim, topped with a tasteless and odorless white sauce squeezed from a frozen bag. There are bargain wines, though, "a taste for every palette."

Bubba Copeland punches Essie Sue. "I thought you got menu choices on a cruise."

"You don't need the extra calories, Bubba. Besides, you get your choice of beverage."

"I get that on a Burger King Special. What if I'm a vegetarian?"

"You're not. And if you are, you can always have the Mashed Potatoes Horatio and the Gardenique Salad. And bread. Who'd want more than that?"

This is some bonus I've won. I can't even imagine having to pay for it. Fortunately, we don't get much time to eat. Just as we've cut into the Sweet Seafood Sorbet, the captain tinkles a glass.

"Welcome one, welcome all."

"All?" Mrs. Steinman from our group breaks in. "Most of them are in the cabins being sick."

"No, no—you're misinformed, madam. This ship is

the most advanced in the Bargain Cruise Line. It's totally stabilized from top to bottom."

"So why is the pharmacy already out of Dramamine?"

"Truly for extraordinary situations—those who have preexisting stomach conditions or perhaps are still recovering from the airline trip. For those passengers, we recommend bed rest."

The only thing worse than showing up for dinner on this ship would be to rest on those beds—the mattresses give the word *firm* a new meaning. Not to mention breathing in the exhaust fumes on our lower deck.

The captain gives one more tinkle on the glass in order to finish his speech. When that doesn't help, his cousin Essie Sue runs one of her remaining fingernails over the microphone. As usual, it works.

"My staff and I aim to please. If anything, I repeat *anything*, is not to your liking, please report it to one of my emissaries in white."

The whole group rises as one—no doubt hoping to mob the emissaries in white, who've unfortunately heard this announcement before, and have disappeared.

11

I can think of several good arguments as to why I should go up on deck to try to find Ed Levinger, but there are dozens of reasons I shouldn't. I didn't see him at the captain's dinner—maybe he's got his own motives for doing a disappearing act. And maybe he's just not enamored of our little temple group—what a thought. At any rate, I think I'll cool it.

There's quite a bit more sailing before we arrive at our destination, but that doesn't stop the compulsive tourists from preparing what's *really* important.

"Do you have your shopping list all planned, Ruby? St. Thomas is good for jewelry." Essie Sue has acquired an enormous tote bag with *Bargain Cruises—More or Less* plastered all over it.

More or Less is right—judging from the price of extras around here—like charging for another roll of toilet paper, the place is run more like a hospital than a bargain boat. I fully expect to be presented with a pair of paper slippers when I leave. Very expensive paper slippers.

"I got this tote bag on sale. It was supposed to say *Bargain Cruises—More for Less,* so now it's only ten dollars instead of twenty. You don't have to pay until you get off the ship. Have you hit the gift shops yet?"

"No, I have a feeling I'll see a few gift shops in St. Thomas on my way to the beach."

"The beach? Why would you go to the beach?"

"Because it's an island, maybe? With beautiful green water? I want to lie on the sand and contemplate my toes. This is my vacation."

"Don't be silly, Ruby. You can take care of your feet at home. And this ship has its own pool."

"You mean that postage stamp–sized hot tub? No thanks. The sight of all those middle-aged bodies vying for position in two square feet of moisture doesn't exactly turn me on. And tonight I saw water sloshing out of it every time the ship rocked."

"Horatio says that's just the ocean waves kicking up— don't pay any attention."

"Okay, I won't." I have to keep reminding myself that all these pleasures are free. I'm suddenly very tired. A conversation with Essie Sue can do that to me.

When she ducks into the ship's third gift shop I make a clean exit. Firm mattress or not, bed is bed, and at least they change the sheets at no charge. Or not. Maybe I'll get a bill at the end of the voyage.

My bedtime reading for the next couple of nights consists of some of the Converso files I printed from Willie Bob's laptop. The material really *is* fascinating, even though I haven't figured out why he called this file "Modern Conversos—Tell Family?"

Imagine living out in the country, being part of a good Catholic community, and finding out at some point that you've been following traditions all your life that not only have no easy explanation, but that are peculiar just to your own kin. Your family, for example, never ate meat with milk, gathered in the fields on a Saturday to socialize, and pulled all the curtains on Friday night while candles were lit—yet you were always known as Catholics and never as anything else. It's just that "Grandmother did it and we all did it, too."

Willie Bob's file contains stories of family groups moving from rural areas to the city and meeting other Catholics who followed the same rituals—mere exercises with little or no explanation attached.

He deals with other questions: When families make these discoveries, how welcome is the information that they might be descended from Sephardic Jews who survived the Spanish Inquisition? Some might not be too thrilled. Gonzales lists names associated with the Spanish Jews, and areas where these groups lived. As sleepy as I am on this last night, when I come across El Paso and a list that contains the name Jacob Marquez, my mind buzzes. Didn't I meet a Sara and Jack Marquez from El Paso at the cocktail party?

I'm yawning, but not too drowsy yet to miss my comfortable mattress and my sweet doggie, Oy Vey. Hope she's doing okay at Milt's house.

I ought to put down these papers and try to pretend this board I'm lying on is a bed. I feel as if I'm beginning to know Professor Gonzales in a different way—not as just one of the many weirdos under Essie Sue's thumb, and a sloshed weirdo, at that, but as a rather compelling scholar. It's terrible he's dead—the one person who could have made this pedantic cruise a unique experience.

12

So much for my day at the beach. The rain is falling so hard out there today, it's coming sideways—at least, I think that's what's happening outside. I wouldn't really know because I'm still on the ship, herded into what looks like another cattle pen. Notes on our doors informed us that our group had to show up this morning by nine for our shore excursions, and now that nine hundred of us are what is optimistically called "lined up," they're letting us loose fifty at a time to be carried by a small cruiser from ship to shore. The ship was supposed to "park" closer to the docks after our long trip—it's anybody's guess why it didn't. With the cruiser taking twenty minutes to load and

unload, this trip to the ship's crowded lounge may be my
only excursion of the day.

I hope some epidemic doesn't break out here—I've
never seen so many people this close since my last San
Quentin movie. They let you have a prison lawyer to
appeal when you do hard time—here they don't even give
you one phone call to your travel agent. And the food's
better in the pen. I'd kill for some hard tack to ward off
that queasy feeling every time the ship rocks. Instead, my
Island Breakfast consisted of a cone-shaped pile of powdered eggs swimming in margarine and topped with a
little Panamanian flag. No bread, but the flag wasn't bad.

I'm finally sprung loose around noon and let out on
shore to explore the capital, Charlotte Amalie. Everyone's
fighting over taxicabs to get out of the rain. So far, I've
managed to avoid Essie Sue and Kevin, and will probably
lose them if I just keep away from the bezillion jewelry
stores. The endless maze of Hilfiger's, Gucci, and Rolex
makes me feel like a Liliputian caught among the pages of
Vanity Fair.

My best and only purchase is a poncho from a street
vendor—it covers everything but my feet. I start up one
of the hills away from the prime shopping area, my new
camera tucked safely into my kidney-shaped shoulder bag.
Now I'm traveling—this is the best I've felt since before
they drew my raffle ticket. These mountainous streets
wind fifteen hundred feet above sea level, so I doubt I'll be
reaching the top, but the narrow lanes are fascinating,
with pastel houses, some centuries old, squeezed onto the

hilltops. The Danes moved into St. Thomas in the seventeenth century, and their architecture shapes the character of Charlotte Amalie. The city map says I'm near the old synagogue, but I'm saving that for tomorrow, when our temple group will tour it.

Rain might be romantic in some situations, but it can really take the pleasure out of sightseeing. Despite the poncho, I feel soaked through, probably because of my wet feet. I'm making my way down one of the streets between Government House and the post office when I see Ed Levinger, also drenched, scrunching his head as far inside the collar of a navy blue windbreaker as he can stuff it. He ducks into a doorway several houses away from me—for shelter, I'm assuming, when I see that it's not a serendipitous stopover. Another figure, carrying a Coach briefcase in British tan, one I've coveted since seeing the smaller size in a shop window here, emerges from the old Lutheran church where I was headed, and joins Ed. That beautiful Coach must be pretty damp. I call out and try to wave and it seems to me that they both take a quick look up, but then they duck into the building. Did they see me? Maybe not.

Now that my attempt at socializing has failed so abysmally, I'm ready to go down to the docks and have a cup of tea. I love these winding streets, but this is no longer fun. I suppose Ed's working on his travel piece— it'd be a lot more fun to see how that evolves than to do the pure tourist bit, but this is *you* on vacation, Ruby— live with it.

I see that I'm not alone in drying out on the water-front—half the ship is here. It's standing room only in the coffee shop, but I'm glad just to get a chance to order at the counter.

"Ruby—over here!"

It was inevitable, I guess. Kevin is sitting with the Marquezes—wonder how they got together. More important, there's a seat between them with nothing on it but umbrellas.

I bring my tea over to the table and make my hellos.

"Where's Essie Sue, Kevin?"

"Oh, she's got one more store to hit—then she's going back to the ship. She invited us all out to the deck for cocktails later."

The outdoor deck? I don't ask. I'm just glad she's not meeting us here.

Jack and Sara Marquez are pleasant enough—obviously part of the country club set in El Paso. And I was wrong—Kevin does know their bishop.

My mind wanders as the three of them discuss Kevin's recent visit to El Paso. I'm sure the fact that his former fiancée, Angel Elkin, was from there won't come up. This conversation sticks to landmark appreciation. The only reason my curiosity is piqued at all is that the name *Marquez* was on Willie Bob's laptop list under *El Paso*. I really want to go over those files.

I wake up to the sound of my name. "Ruby?"

Fortunately, I've had years of clergy wife experience in making fast recoveries at moments like this. It isn't exactly the first time I've gone into a reverie to keep my mind from stagnating.

"Yes?"

"So what do you think about Sara's suggestion?"

"What do you think about it, Kevin? You certainly seem interested." Can't go wrong with that approach—I hope.

"I think it's a great idea."

"I was just telling Rabbi Kapstein, Ruby, that he might increase his attendance at the lectures if he invited some passengers personally each day and arranged to serve a continental breakfast."

Hmm . . . I'm gonna have to improve my act here—I might have fooled Kevin, but obviously not Sara. I'm not used to being around people who think. She does have a great idea, though.

"What a very Jewish thought," I say. "We always depend on food to bring in the crowds."

"With my friends, you'd do better springing for Bloody Marys."

"Jack—you should be ashamed of yourself. We hardly know these people, hon."

Wow—the wife's smart and the husband has a sense of humor—I'm not used to this embarrassment of riches.

"They're giving you good advice, Kevin—go for it. I'm sure the kitchen will help you."

"Oh, I'll just tell Essie Sue—she can get anything she wants."

Sara said continental, not galactic. If he involves Essie Sue, banquets and ice sculptures won't be far behind.

"Let's keep it simple. I'll help you with it."

"I'll be glad to pitch in, too, Rabbi."

"Really, Sara? That means you're coming to hear me tomorrow?"

"Certainly—I'm not averse to learning about other religions."

Yikes—I'd forgotten that helping him serve probably means staying for the lectures. Maybe with Sara there, we can alternate. At any rate, I'd like to get to know her.

A tottering pile of boxes veers toward our little tea table and collapses, causing numerous crockery casualties. Apparently, Essie Sue has lassoed more than just jewelry in her quest for the best on the waterfront. She's probably boosted the island economy by a few percentage points, but before we can hear her report, I offer her my chair as I make a speedy exit. I give Sara a wink so she won't think I'm a complete boor, which I am, of course, and she graciously winks back. Definitely worth knowing.

13

I may have made a clean getaway this afternoon, but I'm not so lucky now.

"This will be a night to remember, people."

Why does my skin crawl whenever I hear that cliché coming out of Essie Sue's mouth? As if my stomach hadn't been churned up enough by the theme dinner at tonight's First Sitting—Taco Fiesta Fantasy. It was no fantasy— even Taco Bell could not have made this up. Real waiters in rainbow vests served trays of real tacos in every color of the rainbow, with fillings to match. You got to choose which colors you wanted placed on your plate—red tacos with chopped-up hot dogs, gray tacos with sardines, or

light green tacos with peas. These were the good colors—
most people declined the blue and the pink on the
grounds of decency, not to mention the yellow.

Essie Sue had put in a special request for Jewish food—
how lucky for us that the kitchen decided to comply on the
very night the food coloring was in abundance. A Korean
chef who claimed to have a Jewish grandmother—don't
ask—made a special presentation at the Temple Rita table,
for which he received copious applause. I decided to rein in
the clapping along with my appetite, until I could assess the
damage.

It was extensive:

Bubbe's Bluehair Brisket—that's *Bubbe,* meaning
"Grandmother"—not Bubba. (In Texas, brisket for Bub-
bas is called barbecue.) In honor of all grandmothers, the
so-called meat was tinged with a blue-gray rinse.

Kosher Kugel Blush—Betty Crocker's Tuna Noodle
Casserole in heavy makeup. Now we know where all
those pink hors d'oeuvres went.

Wandering Julienne—These used to be carrots.

Borscht—Not exactly exclusive to our people, but a
good try. Except that I've never seen a yellow beet, and I
caught a whiff of ginger ale.

There was a silver lining. In keeping with the rainbow
theme, dessert for all the passengers consisted of ten
multicolored M&M's in a paper cup for each person—
definitely the highlight of the meal. Those of us who
weren't sick ate theirs right away.

I figure the whole deal cost fifty cents a person tops, so

it definitely made it on the cost-cutting scale. And that's with the food coloring thrown in.

We survivors are now gathered in Club Blue, the larger entertainment lounge—as if we haven't been treated to enough color already. And this particular all-pervasive teal blue is one of my least favorite colors in the world. But hey, it's a lot better than spending the evening belowdecks. I'm personally here so I won't have to think about the near-hurricane outside, which is making it impossible to carry out my own fantasy. I had actually envisioned moonlit evenings on deck, looking at calm seas. So far I haven't seen the sun, much less the moon.

Our temple group is seated together, awaiting our night to remember, and definitely avoiding ordering coffee—we've been warned the cups might slide off the table and burn us if the room gets any rockier. We have no idea how rocky it's going to get.

The spotlights go on. I won't mention what color they are.

"Ladies and gentlemen, Club Blue is proud to present an Elvis Fantasy." Needless to say, they're big on fantasy here.

Amid very loud drumrolls and a thousand pinpoints of light, one dozen—count 'em—Elvis look-alikes ranging in age from about fifty to past Social Security emerge from the grave (make that crowd) and stand by their appointed tables. But this isn't just live entertainment, or maybe almost live—at the same time the Elvises are taking their bows, slide screens twelve feet tall chronicle the real Elvis's life story, punctuated by roaring but slightly staticky concert tapes.

"Can you believe it, people? It's multimedia!" Essie Sue screams to make herself heard, and unfortunately, we all hear her. "And that's not all—Horatio told me the Elvises will have a contest as to who sounds the most like the real thing."

The Elvises do indeed have a contest. "You Ain't Nothin' but a Hound Dog" is the number of choice—six of the Elvises go with that. The songs are from his early period, but unfortunately the contestants are from his late period.

An hour later, comparing the fake-colored tacos and the all-too-real Elvis look-alikes, I'm hard-pressed to decide which of my senses has taken the most punishment. It's a toss-up. As it is, the room tilts one more time, sending us all to the rails.

14

"All aboard the bus—it's only a short trip."

Short trip is an understatement—Essie Sue has insisted upon a bus to take us from the harbor to our tour destination—only a few blocks at most. Today the ship has crept much closer to shore—we're properly docked at the harbor and don't have to be ferried to land by those slow boats. It *is* raining, though not that hard, so I suppose she has an excuse for using the bus.

"I hope you've all brought bottles of water," she says. "We wouldn't want to have any dehydration problems on our tour today."

Dehydration problems? We're on an island surrounded by water, our ponchos are dripping, we haven't yet seen the sun, and rumor has it that we're in the eye of Hurricane Lenny. The captain's apparently keeping that a secret, and won't let it be mentioned in the ship's newsletter, which has been calling the weather "cloudy" all week. We're definitely in no danger of dying of thirst—in an emergency we can just open our mouths and look up.

"All off the bus."

We've been driving three minutes.

"This is it? I don't see anything—you must have the wrong address," Essie Sue says.

I'm thinking the bus driver has met his match, but I'm wrong.

"This is as close as I'm getting, lady. I don't know why you're going up there, but you're now at the bottom of the old Synagogue Hill, on Crystal Gade. It's too slippery to take my bus up there, and even if I could make it, the streets are so narrow I'd hit something."

"But that's so steep—the ladies will fall backward on their high heels."

"Let's go, Essie Sue," I say as I hop off the bus. "You're the only lady who'd wear high heels on a sight-seeing tour—the rest of us will hold you up. Remember the other morning when we didn't get started until noon? Our touring time is slipping away."

This morning we're visiting St. Thomas's historic Jewish synagogue—something I'm actually looking forward to, despite the wet weather. I even attended Kevin's lecture today, featuring orange juice, sweet rolls, and coffee, all arranged by Sara Marquez. She was right, too—there was a good turnout. We learned that Jews have lived in St. Thomas from 1665, when the island was officially settled, and this congregation was founded by Sephardim, Jews of Spanish heritage, in 1796. The landmark we're touring, the oldest synagogue building in continuous use under the American flag, has been here since 1833.

Our group straggles off the bus and starts up the hill— not an easy climb, I'll admit, but not that bad, either. This is a well-known tourist attraction, so I don't know why the driver wondered why we were going. Probably because Essie Sue was driving him nuts.

"Hi."

I stop on such a steep grade that I almost fall backward into Ed Levinger, but he catches me.

"Well, this is a surprise. I didn't see you on the bus."

"I walked over. Thought I'd join you. I was curious to see what you'll get out of this."

"A lot, I imagine. Have you been here before? I saw you near Government House yesterday, talking to a man who'd come out of that historic Lutheran church."

"Yesterday? I was walking around in the rain, but I can't remember talking to anyone in particular—must have been someone else."

"You didn't see me wave?"

"Now I know it was someone else—if I'd seen you, I'd have come over."

I'm not going to bother mentioning his blue windbreaker, which he's wearing again today. My bagel partner Milt would say, "You're not a lawyer in court, Ruby, and everything's not evidence." Still, I know I saw him. But if he wants privacy, that's okay.

It takes ages for this crowd to trudge up the hill, but we're motivated. We're fighting the rain, too, which is falling faster now. A line of cars is parked on one side, so people use them for support as we climb. I stop to look back at the pink rooftops and little white wooden balconies we've passed on the way. This is a great view down, and I can see more cottages facing us on the other hillside. The tropical rain smells wonderful. Not that I wouldn't like to see it let up, but the extra moisture makes the colors of the flowering bushes more lustrous than ever.

"Soon," Kevin tells us, "we'll be seeing the beautiful entrance to the synagogue, and inside is the famous sand floor." He read about the floor in Willie Bob's files. Those floors are supposed to be symbolic of the biblical forty years in the desert, but it's probable that during the Spanish Inquisition, when Jews were killed for worshiping in public, they scattered sand on the cellar floors, where they prayed in secret. The sand muffled any sounds from rising to the streets above.

I've wanted to ask Ed what he thought of the professor's notes, but he hasn't exactly been accessible. Kevin did tell me Ed helped outline a sample lecture, but aside from that one dance we almost had, I've hardly seen him. And now he says I didn't see him yesterday in the street.

"So where is it?" Essie Sue has given up and put one wet shoe in each pocket of her raincoat. I've never seen her in bare feet except by the pool, but at this moment, she looks pretty happy to be rid of those heels.

"Where's what?" Brother Copeland is panting.

"The temple, of course. It was supposed to be half-way up."

"You're here." Ed Levinger steps in front of us and points to the right.

"That's not the synagogue—that's a construction site," Kevin says. "Someone's building another house and the whole place looks locked up."

"Nope, that's it."

Talk about a man of few words. This is a journalist?

"But this was supposed to be the highlight of our trip," Essie Sue says to the group. Make that *wails* to the group.

"This is gonna spoil my lecture. I was going to give it in front of the Ark made from island mahogany wood, under the imported Baccarat crystal chandeliers. See how much I've learned about this place?"

"I want to see the president of the *shul*," Essie Sue says.

"The president's at home where it's dry," I say. "We're on our own. Let's see how much is torn up. Maybe we can still get in."

The stone steps leading up to the entrance are a beautiful gray-blue slate color, and I'll bet they were locally quarried. I'm slipping all over the place, though, in this driving rain, and my footing is more precarious because of a thick clear plastic sheeting half-draped over some of the steps. When I come to the iron gate at the top of the stairs, it's firmly locked, and posted with official signs reading RESTORATION OF THE ST. THOMAS SYNAGOGUE. Inside the gate, wooden support beams and metal pipes crisscross the construction area, and more of the plastic sheeting flaps in the wind.

"I can't see anything." Kevin's fighting to keep his poncho hood over his head with one hand and hold his lecture notes with the other.

"You ought to put those papers back in your pocket, Kevin," I tell him. "And there *is* something to see here." A large outdoor replica of the Eternal Light with a six-pointed star is above our heads, having survived the construction so far, and some unusual pink brick pillars form a portico at the entrance.

"I know about these bricks, Ruby," Kevin says. "They're rounded bricks handmade in Denmark by special order for the synagogue. Professor Gonzales says the rest of the bricks for this place were from Europe, too— they were used as ballast on the old sailing ships. Then, on the return trips, the ships took back local goods. The mortar holding the bricks together contained molasses, and children in the old days licked the walls to get the sweet taste."

"That's neat, Kevin, but don't just tell me—try to gather everyone around."

"Are you kidding?" Essie Sue's hair is safely tucked under a neat plastic scarf she's made into a turban, but the rest of her is soaked. "We're supposed to stand here and be taught something in this storm? Nothing doing— we're heading down to the bus. We'll visit shops instead."

I guess seeing the synagogue is hopeless from her point of view, but I'd like to poke around a little. I don't mind the rain that much, and since the weather shows no sign of changing, one day's probably as good as another to sightsee.

The group follows Essie Sue—confirming the herd mentality. Why would this be any different from the board meetings she dominates? But I must admit that people seem grateful to be allowed to seek the shelter of the bus.

"Want to stay with me?" I ask Ed before he starts down the hill. "Although I guess you've seen this place on your other visits."

"I did see it before the restoration project—several times, in fact. It's always been one of the major attractions in town. I couldn't figure out why you'd want to see it closed up."

"Well, obviously, we didn't know. You could have said something."

"First, I'm not a part of your group—I just tagged along. I thought you had a special reason for wanting to come."

"I didn't know much about any of this, Ed. It isn't like my usual travels, where the research is as much fun as getting there. But I am catching up—I want to read Kevin's notes in detail. The professor apparently spent a lot of time here. If you worked on Kevin's lecture the other night, you already know that."

"I spent most of our work session writing out the first talk for him, Ruby—he seemed insecure about giving it. That didn't leave much time for looking at Gonzales's other notes."

"Look, Ed—it's still teeming here—you don't have to stay just to keep me company."

"I don't mind staying—I just don't know how much more there is to see, Ruby. What do you want to do here?"

"I don't know yet. I'm really better off exploring by myself—thanks for staying behind when I asked, but I've changed my mind. I'll see you back at the ship, okay?"

"Okay, see you later this afternoon or tonight. I'll look for you. Maybe we can find some decent music in one of the lounges."

"See ya."

I watch the back of his head go lower and lower down the steep hill in front of me. Now that he's gone I'm suddenly lonesome. And feeling very rusty. I hate playing games and I'm not about to start now. Besides, in all fairness, I don't see gamesmanship in anything he's done so far—that's what I like about him. But I don't know him at all. Since we haven't spent real time together, I have no idea what kind of travel piece he's writing—although why should he blab about it? Maybe that's part of his professionalism.

I wish I could fool myself once in a while as other people seem to be able to do, but it ain't gonna happen. Let's face it—I had a chance to be with him today and blew it. We're too much alike—neither of us wants to give an inch. I guess I could have gone down into town with him, or taken up his offer to stay here with me. Of course, he never really *offered* to stay.

15

I'd love to take a look inside here, but the slanted iron gate is locked up tight. In keeping with the angular shape, the sides of the gate are lower than the middle, with iron banisters perpendicular to the entranceway. If I stand on the hand railing, I might be able to swing myself over the lower part of the gate itself and avoid the spiked bars making up the fence. It's worth a try, and with the help of one of the plastic sheets wrapped around the nearest spikes, I manage to slip over the gateway without impaling myself.

The entrance door is firmly padlocked, too, but I now have free access to the courtyard. Who knows—maybe there's an unsecured space on the other side of the building away from the street. I'd say the place is pretty well protected from casual intruders, and the contractors might not have been as cautious with the back section. There's plenty of shrubbery here, too, not to mention the fact that no one else is crazy enough to be out on the street in this downpour, so I don't think I'll be seen.

The arched windows are boarded and barred—looks like I'm not going to be able to look inside—what a bummer. I was hoping the inner restoration might be in an early stage, or a late one, and I could see the benches and floors at least. I'm sure the chandeliers are down and that all the sacred objects have been removed to a safe place. I'm about to go back to the street side when I see a jagged hole in the very top of one of the wooden boards covering a tall window. I'll bet I can stick my camera above my head and take some flash photos of the interior, or better yet, find something to climb on and take a peek myself. Wish I'd brought a flashlight—with this dark day and the blocked windows, there might not be any light at all for seeing this with my own eyes.

Okay. With all this construction debris on the ground, I'd have to be an idiot not to find enough junk to stack up and stand on. We've got pipes, two-by-fours, wooden window frames—in other words, nothing useful, unless I were planning to saw and nail, which I'm not. There's only so far I'm willing to go for a tourist photo. On the other hand, I'd consider it a real coup to break in my new digital camera with a photo no one else could get. Nan would love it, and since I'm now digital, I can e-mail it to her. And if all else fails, I tried. I can't go to the beach, I've already seen part of the town, and I refuse to run from the rain into the waiting arms of a jeweler trying to sell me a gold watch. This is more fun, although I guess I'm alone in that assessment. It wouldn't be the first time.

Why isn't there a ladder here? Do they take them all home at the end of the workday? I see what I think might be a ladder, but it's just a different type of window frame. Over in a corner of the biggest construction pile, though, is a large empty drum of some kind, and it's not heavy. I drag it to the window, place it upside down, and stand on a two-by-four pile to climb up on it. Straddling the rim is going to be safest—I'm afraid the middle might give way.

Damn. There's no way I can look through the hole in the board—it's just too high, and this whole contraption isn't going to last very long. I have good balance at the moment, though, and I can lean against the wall of the building for support, so there's no reason why I can't put the camera up and take my shots above my head. I've got a compact memory card, for extra storage, stuck in the fist I'm using to steady the camera, and my other hand is on the shutter.

I take three rapid-fire shots through the hole. I can see the flash reflecting on the wood, so I know the camera's working. This is great—I'm proud of myself. You're supposed to be able to view these pictures right on the camera through the LCD screen, but I don't dare do it in this weather. Mine is one of the few high-end cameras that contains eight megabytes of internal memory stored in the camera itself, and I've almost used this up with the three photos I've taken.

My balance is still fine, so I slip the compact memory card I'm holding into the camera for more shots through this jagged opening—I want to take a few more of these as well as some shots of the exterior of the building before I leave, and this sixty-four-meg card will give me plenty of room to experiment. Then, whenever I go back to the ship, I can put this memory card into my little computer's PC slot adapter. No developing, no delay. I'll be able to see the results in two places—on the camera's LCD, and in much greater detail on my computer screen.

I've been steadying the drum with my feet all along, just to make sure it doesn't squish too far over in the mud or collapse in the middle. The camera strap is still around my neck, and I carefully ease the camera itself inside the front of my poncho for protection before I climb back down. I was lucky taking those pictures—the rain wasn't quite as heavy as the downpour I'm feeling now.

Should I jump backward or try to kick the drum aside and kind of slide down the wall? If I slide, maybe I can feel with my foot for the pile of two-by-fours I stood on before.

I never get the chance to decide. I hear a rustling behind me and a hollow thump. Before I can turn around or react in any way, I'm suddenly standing on air—the drum's just *gone*. My legs wheel the void for a second as if I'm a character in those *Tom and Jerry* cartoons who plunge off cliffs and keep running. Fortunately, this is no cliff.

I brace my body to fall the few feet down, and try to pull my knees up into a fetal position for a soft landing. This should be a no-brainer—just a roll in the muck. But I don't count on a stunning pain in the back of my head. It's the last thing I feel.

16

The dense tropical rainstorm turns out to be a blessing. I would have been out much longer without those needlelike drops hitting my face. As it is, I don't think I lost consciousness for more than a couple of minutes. I could be wrong, of course—my brain isn't exactly functioning on all burners. My head must have hit a board or a pipe as I fell, although I can't figure out how—I didn't drop all that far, and my body was curled to fall forward or sideways. Instead, I have a whammer of a headache and a big bump on the back of my scalp. No blood, though—thanks to the thick Temple Rita baseball cap I had on under the poncho. I discovered the other day that the cap's bill was great for keeping the rain out of my eyes.

I'm able to ease myself up partway with my hands, spread my legs out for balance, and just sit. I don't know how long I'm in a funk, but it doesn't much matter—I'm incapable of doing anything else. When my eyes focus I look at my watch and see that it's just past noon. I was right—I wasn't out for very long. The headache's a bitch, but it feels much better when I don't move. Even looking at my watch made it hurt more. Despite that, I decide to delicately wiggle my arms and legs to see if disaster's struck anywhere else. It hasn't. I guess I'd rather have my head hurt than to have a sprained ankle on my vacation.

Oy. My vacation. I'm gonna kill that Milt—of all people, he shouldn't have encouraged me. Not that this particular predicament is anyone's fault but mine. I've taken risks for years just to get unusual photos, so I guess the imaging karma finally caught up with me—make that digital imaging. My heart gives a sudden *schreck,* as they say in Yiddish, as I feel for the camera around my neck and don't find it, but I see that it has rolled under some overhanging boards. I hold my head with one hand, grit my teeth to ward off the pain, and reach for it. Whew—it's in a fairly dry space. There is a photography god, after all. I'll kill myself if the camera's broken—these digitals are like little computers, at computer prices, not to mention losing the hard-earned photos I took earlier. It still turns on, so I guess all is well, and the parts look the same as before I fell.

I put the camera back around my neck and under the poncho before I make the big attempt to stand up. Thank heavens the place is deserted—this maneuver isn't pretty. I roll over on my knees in the mud and get up on all fours, then it's sheer grit from there as I get my balance through the pain and rise up like a phoenix—or more accurately, a wounded rhino.

I make an instant decision to come back another time to take photos of the building's exterior—I might be demented, but not suicidal. It'll be all I can do to walk down the hill and travel the few blocks to where the ship's docked. If I'm lucky, the driving rain will wash me off and I'll resemble all the other soaked wretches roaming these streets—except that they're carrying wet shopping bags, and I'm not.

What's keeping me going is curiosity about what my flashbulbs illuminated inside the old synagogue, but I have to admit that every part of me aches. I don't think my vision is blurred, but it's hard to tell when you're looking through raindrops. The streets are deserted as I lumber down the hill to the docks, and I'm able to slip onboard and show my ship's pass without having to speak to anyone. The passengers are either out shopping or home hitting the slots, I suppose. It's a good day for a nap, too—exactly what I aim to do.

I'm sick of water, but that doesn't mean I can avoid showering. Since our cabins are the lowest level in every sense of the word, showering in them is a back-to-basics event—like water trickling from a spiked tin can. The sprinkler is a handheld unit that dispenses next to nothing. Fortunately, the piece of imported soap from Bangladesh doesn't lather, either, so everything's balanced out. I would have done better with wet towelettes. I've brought my good shampoo from home, and I try to clean the bump on my head without actually touching it—a neat feat. Rinsing my hair is so pitiful I actually have to use a liter of bottled water to get the suds out, but reaching for anything in the bathroom is a breeze—this shower stall is more like an elevated shelf. Turning around in it is out unless you're three years old or under.

I put on shorts and a tee shirt and I'm ready to throw myself on the bed when I remember how much that would hurt on this mattress, so I sit down carefully instead. In fact, I don't lie down at all—I'm afraid of a worse headache. Besides, I'm not very sleepy and I have more interesting things to do. I put the little Toshiba computer on the cot with the camera beside it and my directions, too, just in case. Not that the camera instructions were ever printed up by the manufacturer—that's now passé. You'd think that the camera would be bundled with a handbook, but all help is now on-line. Only the cheap cameras have instructions. If you want hard copy, you damn well better save the hundred or so pages on a disk and take it to Kinko's to be printed and collated. Which is exactly what I did before leaving on this trip.

I carefully wipe off every exposed part of my camera— aside from one nick on a corner, it's dirty, but okay. My heart's pounding, though, as I turn it on. I checked it out briefly in the synagogue yard, but only to see if the power worked. The insides are a different story. Yeah, all the complex little menus flash on the LCD screen, which has miraculously escaped scratching—I see one faint mark at the edge, but that's all. Then I do a double take. A flashing screen screams at me in all caps—OUT OF MEMORY: NO MEMORY CARD INSTALLED.

Well, I know I'm out of memory in the camera itself—that eight megs of internal memory was used up by the three photos I took of the interior. But the screen shouldn't be saying I'm out of memory at all. Once I stuck the little sixty-four-meg compact flash memory card in, any memory problems would have been taken care of.

At first, I think there's a screw-up with the camera workings—maybe the computer program mechanism did get corrupted when I fell and isn't registering the card's presence. There's a tiny hinged cover on the bottom of the camera, covering the slot where I inserted the memory card. I push it open and find good news and bad news. The good news is that there's nothing wrong with the camera— the indicators were accurate when they flashed the out-of-memory warning. The bad news, of course, is that the slot is empty.

I go over every step in my mind. I know I inserted the card and closed the cover before I fell. I also know that when I picked up the camera from its dry space under the pile of wood, everything was in place. It would have been perfectly obvious if the cover had been knocked open during the fall—it would have been hanging by the hinges. And it's highly unlikely if that *had* happened that the memory card itself would have fallen out—it fits snugly in its slot. Not that it's impossible, but if the card did drop out, the cover would have opened first, and would have been that way when I found the camera. Also, when I checked and cleaned everything just now, the cover was closed.

So where's the card?

17

I'm usually pretty good at objective analysis—at pulling something apart, sorting it, and putting the pieces back together in some logical order. But this afternoon I feel— well, I feel like someone who's fallen on her head. I want to think clearly, but nothing makes any sense. I've traced and retraced the events of this morning in chronological order, and that's not working, so I've now decided to begin at the end. The last fact is not quite believable to me—the memory card is missing from my camera, but it couldn't have dropped out by accident. That being said, I have to hypothesize that someone took it out of the camera and closed the cover. Who, why, and when?

It wasn't an ordinary thief because, in that case, the whole expensive camera would be gone, and so would my money. So this not-so-ordinary thief observed that I was using a digital camera and reasonably assumed that the photos I had taken were stored on electronic film, which in this case happens to be the compact memory card. This person took the card so that he or she could have the photos on it, or so that I *couldn't* have them. Only I knew that the card was empty and ready to record the exterior shots I was planning to take at the front of the building.

I feel dizzy, but it's only the ship rocking violently in this increasingly ugly weather. I pull the covers around me for at least the illusion of security, and hold tight to my camera. The phone rings.

"Ruby, this is Essie Sue. What in the world happened to you? When we got back to the bus, we did a head count and you weren't there. Meet us for cocktails on deck in an hour."

As usual, she doesn't wait for answers—that would involve listening skills.

"I can't, Essie Sue. I'm seasick. 'Bye."

This kills me because I've prided myself on not getting sick even once, but it's just too obvious an excuse not to use it. I don't want to show up with bruises and a cocked head—the bump feels better when my head's tilted, for some weird reason. More important, I don't want people being alarmed that something happened to me until I can at least figure out what it was.

I hate being a victim—yuck. If I'm seasick, everyone

will leave me alone—misery might love company, but company does not love misery, especially if the miserable one is about to throw up. There's something about nausea that demands instant respect, or at least a wide berth.

Almost instantly, the phone rings again. Are these people that organized?

"Ruby, it's Ed. I looked for you in town around lunchtime—I figured you couldn't have been poking around in that construction mess for very long—the rain was getting worse."

"Yeah, I came back to the ship, Ed, and made the mistake of trying to take a nap in this cabin. I woke up seasick."

Essie Sue was one thing, but this *really* hurts.

"Join the crowd—half the ship's under. It's no fun, though—can I bring you something?"

"No, I just need to rest."

"Since you're not sleeping well anyway, can I call you tonight? Maybe you'll feel better if you're up and walking. Or if we're lucky, the rain will let up and you can walk the outside deck for a few minutes."

"Okay, but why don't I call you instead? You gave me the room number the other day—I'll leave a message if I'm feeling better."

I should probably have told him what's going on, but I don't know him that well. For all I can tell, he'd be reporting this to the cops, and I'm not ready for that yet. Maybe I *am* suffering some effects from that bump. All I need is to be grilled when I haven't worked everything out to my own satisfaction yet. A good night's sleep might make all the difference.

Back to the groaning board. It does not please me to realize that having figured out the *why* of this morning's episode, the *when* is not far behind. I vaguely remember a noise behind me and a hollow thump. If the thief wanted the camera contents, he got them by kicking the drum out from under me and knocking me on the head. He'd have to, because the camera was safely strapped around my neck and under my poncho. It would only take a few seconds to yank the camera from my neck, pull out the card, and close the memory cover so the camera would appear untouched long enough for me to at least suspect I had fallen off the drum and hit my head in a careless accident. I was so relieved to see the camera all in one piece that I never even thought about the card until this afternoon. Which was exactly the point.

Now I've got to see whatever it was that I captured on those photos still remaining in the camera's internal memory. Anyone else would have tried to look at them right away, but with me, first things first. That compact flash card is worth in dollars a few hours' computer consulting work for me back home, and I still can't believe it's gone. At least it didn't have any photos stored on it—the thief got *zilch*.

When I turn on the LCD camera monitor I'm sickened to see that the first two images are dark—total duds. Maybe something will show up when I transfer them to the larger laptop—not that it's much bigger, since the

Toshiba is somewhere in size between a handheld and a regular laptop, but the screen is good. The third image, though, looks promising. Since it's stored in the internal memory I have to transfer it by slow serial cable to the Toshiba, but it's only one photo, so it doesn't take long. The flash worked well, apparently, and has illuminated *something* inside the renovation site. I'm just not sure what it is. I've seen pictures of the interior before the renovation, but this scene bears little resemblance to any of those. At least I've now found all those ladders I was looking for on the ground when I was trying to peek into the building—they're stored here along with construction machinery and building materials.

I guess Ed was right—there's nothing to see in here—the construction has enveloped everything. My best bet, photographically speaking, is to go back before we sail and take pictures of the outside brick columns and stonework, and get a shot of the gate.

I try to transfer the two dud photos to the Toshiba, too, just to make sure I don't miss anything, but I get total black. The third one is all I've got, and I put it back on the screen for a last look before storage. Of course, what did I expect from a shot taken from above my eyes and through a hole in the wood? Still, I was conked over the head for this, so it's worth something to me.

The photo-editing program on my computer has an enlargement feature. I divide the image into four sections and take a long look at each quadrant. The angle of the shot is so skewed to begin with that it's hard to tell where the horizon lies, and dividing this jumble into parts makes any analysis that much more difficult. Some objects are in focus and some horribly out of focus. As a tourist photo, this image is definitely a throwaway. I finally figure out where the floor is, or what's left of the floor space. As I'm examining the farthest corner of the bottom-right section of the picture, almost out of camera range, I do a double take.

There, in surprisingly good focus, nestled between three tin pails and a huge shovel, a briefcase stands upright. Not just any briefcase—a new one in British tan. I isolate the image and enlarge it to another degree, just to make sure I read the word *Coach* right.

18

First of all, don't panic at anything in this letter—just do everything I ask you. Having a less than wonderful time.

I know you're probably surprised to hear from me twice this week, and if you're back by now from visiting your mom, you might even get both my e-mails at once. Read the other one first—that fills you in on everything. I'm writing this one from the same hotel Internet

café as I did last time—so glad I discovered it. It has computers for use as
well as a line to plug into a local phone
number.

Yesterday I was trying to take some
photos of the old temple I mentioned and
am pretty sure I was mugged, of sorts. I
was knocked over the head and the memory
card from my digicam was stolen. I'm fine
now, just have a sore bump on my scalp,
which hurts much less today.

I won't go into all the reasons, but
I'm sure the mugging was not random, and
because of that, I'm sending you as an
attachment a graphics file of a photo I
took. It's dark, jumbled, and distinctly
untouristy, but I want you to keep it
on your computer for me, and also to
print it out on your new photoprinter.
I've already erased the image from my
camera, and I'm transferring this computer copy of the file to a Zip disk,
which I'll also erase as soon as I hear
from you that you've received the photo.
I don't feel safe carrying any of the
images around. I'm hoping the thief
thinks the rain and low light kept me
from getting an image on my camera—I
doubt he or she would know it was held in
the camera's internal memory. At any
rate, it's not there now—as I said, I got
rid of it.

Last night I declined some invita-
tions—said I was seasick instead of
telling anyone what happened—and stayed

in my cabin. I went through the files I had backed up from the professor's laptop—the heart attack victim I told you about. No definite theories, but there's a lot fishy going on here besides the slimy creatures sloshing on deck from the hurricane! I know you'd tell me I was jumping to conclusions, but I think maybe Willie Bob Gonzales, or a person with access to his files, was blackmailing someone. He'd discovered that some of these prominent Texas Christians had Jewish roots, and he'd even planned to schedule meetings with them. It sounds benign enough, but who knows that everyone would be so thrilled to get the news, or have it spread around?

Maybe my photo op gone awry is casting a sinister pall on everything I read in his files, but I think my theory's worth looking into, and I'm not losing the chance to do it. Willie Bob makes reference to a password several times, but I can't find it. There's enough in these files to make me wonder about his sudden heart attack, too. How about calling our friend Lieutenant Paul Lundy long distance from Seattle and asking him to do some background checks for me? He owes us, which means you'll have to convince him to trust my decision not to bring in the police here—I think I was mugged, but I'm not sure enough to go public yet.

> Tell Paul to look at the Houston or
> Galveston medical examiner's reports on
> the professor's body. And while you're
> at it, I e-mailed you about the cute guy
> I danced with at the captain's recep-
> tion—Ed Levinger. Can you find out from
> the Net or by some phone calls if he's
> written articles for the San Antonio
> papers? And what kinds of articles?
> Back into the storms and tides—love, me

This café has great Lapsang souchong tea—hot and smoky—perfect for a rainy day and a sore head. I'm scated by the window, absorbing all the light I can get in the midst of this monsoon—it looks like the Pacific Northwest in late December. Imagine my cheek to think I'd be using tons of sunblock and slurping tropical ices on this trip.

I save my photo file to the Zip disk and erase it from my hard drive, and I put the disk in the travel pouch inside my shirt pocket holding ID documents and traveler's checks. With luck, it won't be there long, and I'll hear from Nan tomorrow that she received the file. I could call her tonight, but calls from the ship are horribly expensive, and I just feel better not using its facilities if I don't have to.

I could do some of this Internet research myself, but I'm paranoid about who might walk into this café. This way, I can check in every day—or at least as long as the weather precludes the beach excursions. I don't want to appear to be a total hermit, though, so if I feel okay, I plan to partake tonight in whatever. I pull out the daily schedule. The weather is still cloudy, except that the cloudy forecast has been replaced by *low* clouds. Yeah, low like we're inside them. Tonight we're having Las Vegas Night—the opportunity to win a fortune, the captain writes. *Oy.* There's not a chance in hell our group would miss this.

A yellow poncho walks into the café with Kevin's eyeglasses peeking out of it.

"Look what I checked out of the ship's library, Ruby."

"I didn't know we had a ship's library."

Kevin squishes down on the seat across from me and reaches for my tea.

"Can I have some? Yeah, we have a library, but it only has a dozen books—you check them out on the honor system, and the passengers contribute their old paperbacks."

Sounds like Bargain Cruise Lines.

"I found this paperback on blackjack and other games of chance—isn't that great?"

"Great is where you find it, I guess. Can I have my tea back?"

"Phew—it smells awful."

"Then why not order your own, Kevin?"

That was a mistake—I don't want to sit here this long.

"Essie Sue says our group is getting free tokens courtesy of her cousin—you can play them in certain slot machines. Then you swap them for prizes."

"Is that the opportunity to win a fortune?"

"I guess. Listen, Ruby—I've been wanting to ask you a favor. My lectures are going over so well, Essie Sue says I should give three more—especially since the weather's bad and people are staying on the ship. Would you help me again?"

"Why not ask Ed to write them? He's a journalist."

"I did ask him, but he didn't seem interested. He kept the laptop overnight that night he helped me, just to see if there was anything else we could write about. Since he didn't find anything then, I doubt he'd want to start searching all over now. But I know you can find something—there's lots of material in there."

"You didn't tell me he kept it overnight."

"You didn't ask—you didn't even come to my first lecture the next morning, remember?"

"I'm sorry, Kevin—I really needed to catch up on my sleep. Okay, I'll help you. Give me the key to your cabin and I'll look at the laptop this afternoon while you're out. Maybe I can outline another lecture for you. If I finish before you're back, I'll take your key to my room and you can come get it."

"Thanks, Ruby. This is working out great for me— Essie Sue says I'm proving myself. I don't have to tell the class you wrote it, do I?"

"I'd be shocked if you did, Kevin. See you later."

He can have the credit, if I can have his key.

Can't wait to look at that laptop.

19

I won't say I'm sneaking into Kevin's cabin, but I'm being very careful that no one sees me. That experience at the synagogue left me with a healthy amount of paranoia. Outlining another lecture for him won't take much effort with all that material available, and I'm just curious to see what it was that Ed wrote for him. I search through the files and notice an unfamiliar one—it must be Ed's. He's done a very thorough job of outlining a talk on Jewish symbols and practices that have filtered down to modern-day Converso families. *Watered* down would be a better description—practice without meaning can be a weird phenomenon. It must have seemed strange in a rural household to have a family *habit,* really, of meeting in the fields on Saturday mornings, yet not knowing why. I can definitely tell Ed's a writer—this looks very professional.

Well, no secret little notes revealing Ed's life and times. Of course, if I truly want to know about him, I ought to be able to conjure up a better way than peeking in computers—spending some time with the man might be a teeny bit more efficient. What was he doing with that man near Government House the other day, and why did the guy's briefcase appear in the middle of my picture?

Outlining Kevin's lecture takes very little time, and I doubt he'll be back this soon. I'm sure he wants to give me plenty of time—he's pretty canny when it comes to his own best interests. I decide to check out the document properties connected to Willie Bob's files, just to see if the statistics list the last time the documents were saved or modified—which would be the night I used my Zip disk to back up the files. The date's in there as I thought it would be, but it's superseded by another date—the next day at about two in the morning. So these files were saved after they were out of my hands, and certainly Kevin had nothing to do with it. His knowledge of computers consists of looking at the note I wrote him on how to turn the computer on. He definitely doesn't know how to save anything.

I'm attempting to look up another document I found

interesting last night when I was examining my Zip disk backup files, and I can't find it. I recheck the name where it's stored in my own computer, and still can't locate it on Willie Bob's laptop. I try several more files—one concerning the list from El Paso with the Marquez name on it, and another that was a mysterious reference to passwords. None of these is on the laptop. Ed must have erased some of these files. I do a quick count of my own backup files on the Zip and compare them with the total files on the laptop. A good third of those are gone.

I wonder if Ed looked in the properties section as I did—if he didn't, and he might have had no good reason to think of it, then he doesn't know I backed up the whole megillah. The fact that he erased so many of the files tells me he might not have noticed my backup— otherwise, why bother to get rid of what he knows I have? My hunch is that he figured I might have read some of the files in passing, but that I wouldn't remember how many there were or ever look them up again. He knew I only spent an hour or so with Kevin that evening, because Kevin had a date in Ed's room at eleven. Most of my time would have been devoted to writing the lectures. He has no idea that while Kevin was having the pages printed in the ship's business office, I ran back to my room and copied all the files—no one knows that.

So, Mr. Sweetcheeks, what's up?

I've got a problem here. If I don't keep my interest

in check, I could blurt out the wrong thing and never get anything out of him again. I'll also be a lot more informed if I wait to hear from Nan—I wonder if I conveyed the proper sense of urgency to her? I guess I'll just have to depend on the uncanny ESP we have—she's certainly going to be worried enough about my getting hurt yesterday. In fact, I can imagine her on the phone with our police lieutenant the minute she reads my e-mails. Let's hope so, anyway. I need to know who Ed Levinger is.

So what do I do tonight at the casino—avoid him again?

My heart does a flip-flop when someone knocks at the door.

"Ruby? Are you still in there?"

Whew. "Hold on, Kevin—I'm in the bathroom."

I put my computer back in its case and find the lecture I was working on in the laptop. Then I let him in.

"You're still here—that must mean you're really into my lectures. Did you do all of them?"

"Nope—just the one. I did outline some points you can make for the others."

I could grill him about Ed's taking the laptop overnight, but what's the use? He's probably told me all he knows, and I don't want him talking about it when we're all together.

You'd think he'd ask about the work I did for him, but as usual, he's perfectly content to take the notes with him to class and read from them word for word.

I remind him it's just an outline, but he's no longer interested.

"I'm ready for the gambling tables tonight, Ruby— I've been studying that paperback on how to beat the odds."

"What gambling tables? The whole casino's crammed together in that little room off the dining area. This might be Las Vegas Night, but believe me, Kevin, it's not the real thing. If you've been through there, you can see it's mostly slot machines."

"Of course I've been through there—we have to walk through it on our way to dinner. Still, it's more than we have in Eternal."

"Four movies in one place is more than we have in Eternal. Still, just talking about the place makes me homesick."

"I can't believe you're homesick in the midst of all this luxury, Ruby. Who'd think we'd ever be cruising the blue Caribbean?"

"Olive green, if you haven't noticed. I'd kill for a glimpse of blue waters."

"The captain says this is just a little squall—it'll be over in a few days."

"The trip will be over in a few days, too."

"Ed Levinger was asking for you upstairs."

"Did you tell him I was down here?"

"No. Since he wouldn't help me, I decided to let him see what I could do on my own."

"Don't you mean what we could do on *our* own?"

"Whatever."

Whatever indeed. I couldn't care less about Kevin's duplicity, but I'm thrilled that it caused him to keep quiet about my afternoon date with the laptop.

20

The *Bargain II*'s social director must be geographically challenged or a tad confused—either way, we're all being favored with Hawaiian leis around our necks as we enter the late-night Las Vegas Night party. Essie Sue, resplendent in a long floral print, which is also strangely Hawaiian—she must have had advance warning—is handing out our special group bonuses.

"This is what comes from being in with the power structure, people. You can thank my cousin Horatio for these complimentary cocktail tickets and free slot machine tokens."

Bubba Copeland waves a pale iced drink in her face. "If

this is an example of the free cocktails, count me out. I tried to take my ticket to the bar and the guy told me I needed to go to the card table in the corner to get my freebie. This is it—can you taste any alcohol?"

"What do you want for nothing, Bubba? You of all people don't need any encouragement with hard liquor. Just be appreciative of all these group privileges."

There's also a special slot machine for our free chips. We can swap the bounty for plastic combs, sewing kits in a thimble, and bow-tie barrettes. Whoopie.

"Count your blessings, people. My cousin the captain tells me the cruise line is strapped for money. You passengers have no idea of the problems with plumbing, food supplies, and good help, so I'd say they were being very generous in giving us anything."

"Please, Essie Sue." Bubba's brother, Brother, tosses his barrette in her lap. "As a paying passenger, I'm all too aware of problems with the plumbing and food supply. When the Dramamine tastes better than lunch, the problems are obvious. Not to mention taking ten minutes for the toilet to flush."

"They're coping, Brother. Don't spoil this elegant evening. Especially since our benefactor is heading this way with his entourage."

Talk about a big fish in a little sea. I wonder which galley slave has to starch and iron those spotless uniforms. This emperor definitely has no clothes problem—it's everything else that's missing.

Uh-oh. He's veering toward me.

"Swept up in our fabulous festivities, Ruby? You must be thinking this is a far cry from little Texas. Life's dreams have been fulfilled on my cruises, trust me."

I heave silently. Humility must run in the family. You'd have to be a real loser to trust this guy with anything—much less your life's dreams or any question concerning the states of the Union. I hope there's no veiled hint that he's thinking of fulfilling something connected with me.

"All of us from the tiny state of Texas are just bowled over, Captain. Pardon me for a minute—I need to find a railing."

"Ruby, come back here." I think that's Essie Sue's voice, but I'm halfway to the outside deck already. It's not raining, believe it or not. On the other hand, I won't say it's windy out here, but all evidence of gravity has disappeared.

I'm trying to hold on to the railing when I'm literally blown back into a pair of very strong arms. As long as they're not the captain's or Kevin's, I'm grateful. Two days ago I'd even have been intrigued, but tonight the fact that they belong to Ed only throws me into a double dilemma. What's a nice Jewish boy named Levinger doing near that leather briefcase I was mugged for trying to photograph? And why didn't he come back to the synagogue that day to check on me? What's worse, maybe he did.

"Ruby Rothman—fancy catching you here. What happened—is Las Vegas Night sending you overboard already, or are you just nauseous?"

"Cute, Levinger. That could have come out of my own

mouth. Actually, I haven't decided whether I'm going all the way over the rail or not. This weather isn't improving my frame of mind, either. Were your other trips to the islands like this?"

"Never. This is the all-time pits, hurricane-wise. We're on the outer edge of the storm, I hear, so we're taking the worst battering."

"I thought they steered these ships away from storms."

"They're supposed to, but this particular captain breaks the mold, if you haven't caught on to that already. He's so obsessed with being king of the sea that no one can tell him anything. Another couple of days ought to convince him, though."

"You're kidding, right? Two more days and we'll *all* be ready for the loony bin—or the infirmary. My gut tells me to stay away from that infirmary—it looks lethal."

"Your gut would be right. I'd rather use a snake oil remedy than set foot in there. Have you been seasick? I can tell you what to do about it."

"No—I'm one of the few passengers on this ship who hasn't."

Whoops—I gave that one away. This guy gets me so flustered I'm not on my game—maybe he won't notice.

"So how come you told me you were ill when I called your cabin yesterday?" he says.

"I simply didn't feel like being social. I'd just told Essie Sue the same thing when she called, and it worked with her."

"Gee, thanks. I thought I might rate a little higher than

the Obnoxious One. I was concerned about you—I called earlier and got no answer, and I wondered if you were still tramping around that construction site in the wind and rain."

"Speaking of wind, couldn't we find another place to have this skirmish? It's not fun trying to keep my balance and parry with you at the same time."

"That's just because you're losing and desperate to change the subject. But yeah, I do know a better place. Let's go down to the lower deck—there's a partially glassed-in section where we can be outside but protected from the wind."

I'm ready to spit as we head down the stairwell. How is it that I'm the one getting the grilling and losing, when he has so much to answer for? Damn—if I were just ready to ask those questions tonight. Until I hear more from Nan, I'm gonna have to squelch every bit of competitive spirit.

By the time we reach the lower deck, I've decided on my game plan. This can be get-acquainted night—we really haven't had much chance to talk, considering the company we keep. I'm willing to talk about myself as long as I make sure he reciprocates—I need to find out a lot more about him before I can decide who I'm dealing with. If I didn't have these nagging doubts, he'd be the one person here I'd want to confide in about my experience the other day. Journalists are used to working around the police, and I could use some of his know-how. He's also familiar with the island.

On the other hand, if he's smack in the middle of this and I blab, I've had it. Making sure the conversation focuses on our mutual résumés ought to keep me from blurting out anything I shouldn't. Although I keep being thrown off track by those direct green eyes of his.

After we settle into two comfortable chaises in a corner of the covered deck, I decide to fire first this time.

"Can I ask you something, Ed? How come you're such a wise-ass tonight, when you've been practically mute the rest of the trip?"

"I gather you like me better mute."

"Not on your life, but that's beside the point. You're just so abnormally quiet most of the time, and I wondered why."

"Abnormally quiet, huh. Are you always this blunt? It's refreshing, but more like a pail of ice water in the face. Being quiet is my reporter mode. Not my interviewer mode, where you need to be personable to get anything out of someone."

"So which is you?"

"Neither. They're my work. What you call quiet is just my way of observing—until I see how the pieces fall out."

"It's not the first time I've been called blunt. And I can turn on the socialization if I have to."

"Well, I hope you don't do it for my sake. I'd rather have blunt."

"Maybe *abnormal* was a little much. Essie Sue could squelch anyone."

"I don't see you feeding her conversational tidbits,

either, Ruby. You're pretty detached around these people, too, in case you haven't noticed."

"Let's just say they don't bring out the *me* in me."

So what am I accomplishing here? Not only am I messing up my own interview mode, but I'm feeling much too close to my subject. He does that to me.

"Exactly what kind of reporting do you do?"

"I work for the daily. Do you know San Antonio?"

"Not well—for a place that's only an hour or so away, I've spent very little time there."

"Maybe you could come down sometime. We could have dinner on the River Walk. Would you be interested?"

Now I'm flustered—this is not the conversational turn I was expecting. This is what I get for basically not looking at men since Stu died—I'm rusty. I'm definitely not ready to think of going out with this guy, even if he is exactly the type I'd like to dive into the dating pool with. And I don't know how to cleverly hold everything in abeyance until I *am* ready. Shit.

He shifts around so that he's facing me a bit more. I liked it better when we could both stare out at the ocean.

"Are you wondering if I'm just in interview mode?"

"I'm wondering why you'd even consider *being* in interview mode, Ed. I'm not article material."

"Neither am I, Ruby. So why do I get the feeling you're taking mental notes on all my answers?"

"You think I'm interviewing?"

"It takes one to know one."

I've got to hand it to him—he's playing my game better than I am. I guess I *was* interviewing him.

"Touché. But you know, you haven't even told me if you're just a travel writer. Or how well you really knew Willie Bob Gonzales. Kevin was curious as to why you kept the laptop overnight."

"The rabbi's not curious about anything, Ruby—think of something better."

"I'm thinking we should go inside before we both blow it."

"Just when the armor was finally coming off. Are you sure?"

"I'm sure you haven't given me one straight answer yet."

"Yeah, but the questions are getting more interesting."

I can't believe we're both snickering at that. Ed jumps up and reaches out a hand to help me. I do it myself, although I don't spring up as well as he did.

"If we find some music, will you dance with me, Ruby, or is that up for grabs, too?"

"Is what up for grabs?"

"Us."

I'm already halfway to the inside door, pretending I didn't hear that. It's late enough so that I can beg off and go to bed without much fanfare. Dancing with him right now is not something I need to do. It could be a diversion from the hard questions, but I don't think I'm ready to be so close on the dance floor—my sense of smell can't take whatever it is he's always deliciously giving off.

I might not have dated for a while, but I do remember that this nose of mine has always been my primo essence-indicator. You can give me a fine face, a first-rate mind, and even a great body, but if the aroma doesn't fit, forget it. It's the ancient olfactory sense, I guess. I'm not talking extremes here, either—it's something more subtle than a bad odor or a good cologne. The skin makes the match, and if it's not right, it's not right. When it is, I'm more than halfway there. Which is why I need to get away before I'm tempted.

21

I'm off the ship early this morning—for a couple of reasons. One, I ought to be hearing from Nan today, and two, I don't want to run into any of my shipmates if I can help it—especially my boy Ed. Any ordinary person would have lost interest by now, but he's too smart to think this is just some dating game I'm playing. Last night's fiasco made it perfectly clear that I was running for cover—at least for a while. When we came inside from the outer deck, I made some quick conversation with our temple group and just waved him off with a "See you tomorrow."

It's also not lost on him, I'm sure, that I'm suspect of

his interest in me. I should never have dropped that remark about Ed's keeping the laptop overnight—it was too early for that when we're both still at the stage of dancing around each other. And underlying it all is some fairly obvious chemistry, which complicates everything.

I'm fairly inhaling the Internet café's Island Coffee— which island that is, I don't know and don't care at the moment—I'm just grateful it's bringing me back to life. I didn't sleep well last night, surprise, surprise, and combined with the fact that I'm not a morning person, I practically crawled over here from the docks. I wave away the waitress's offer of food (a clear indicator I'm obsessed) and log on to the Internet right away.

Yes! She's here.

E-mail from: Nan
To: Ruby
Subject: *Watch Your Ass*

Ruby, you're out of control. I can tell the symptoms halfway across the hemisphere. Is it really making you feel better that the police in Texas know about your getting conked on the head when the local cops who can actually help you don't know at all? I don't get it why you didn't report this, although I can certainly understand why you're not telling anyone yet. I don't think you should talk to any civilians until

you know who's who or what's what. But
that's what's bothering me—I hate to see
you operating totally solo—this is not
smart.

I spoke to Lieutenant Lundy and he
gives the same advice—get the local
police involved. Paul contacted Galveston and we're in luck, sort of. Since the
corpse was brought in from a disembarkation site, there's more red tape
involved than if the death had occurred
in someone's home. There's also a pro-
cessing backup for administrative reasons having nothing to do with this
case, and that's meant that the permission for burial has been held up. Paul
has a friend down there who's going to
flag the body for a closer look—if it's
even been examined at all yet, which he
doubts.

Okay. On the other front, Ed Levinger
is one of San Antonio's active investigative reporters for the leading
paper—his byline is all over their
archives. I called a friend there and
she knows his name—says he's tops. It's
possible that he does travel pieces, but
I couldn't find any in my search.

I received the e-mail attachment of
your graphics file and it's stored safely
on my computer and on a Zip disk. I also
printed out a hard copy on my photo
printer, and I must say, it's not one
of your finer efforts. Looks like it was
taken from a helicopter flying sideways—

ha. The only thing that's really in focus is a briefcase, which you seem to have zoomed in on—how did you do that? The rest of the room looks like a bunch of junk, which is probably fine, since it's all out of focus anyway. But you can relax—I've got it.

Now, answers from your first e-mail—sorry the trip's turned out to be such a bummer—crossing my fingers the weather will change and you'll get to the beach. I know what a water baby you are, and I'd hate to see you disappointed. As for the new guy, I haven't seen you this inter- ested in ages—it'd be great to see you come back to life—about time. Since he seems legit as a reporter, why not con- fide in him about this?

I have other things to tell about my life in the dull lane, but I know you're anxious to hear about this more impor- tant stuff, so I'll send immediately, and will be on the lookout for your next e-mail.

Be careful, Ruby . . . please? Not that I think my entreaties will do a bit of good.

Love, Me

That's funny—she thinks I was actually *after* that brief- case in the photo—she should only know how I climbed up to take it over my head. I'm lucky it came out at all—

and now at least I know it's safe, for whatever that's worth. Her advice about confiding in Ed might be good, except for one problem—when I e-mailed her about him I had no idea he'd erased files from the professor's laptop. I'm glad he has a good rep as an investigative reporter, but why would he destroy files that don't belong to him? Something more has to be going on.

I can't wait to find out about the medical examiner's report—the more I'm into this mess, the more I wonder about that sudden death. Thank heavens for Nan.

I'm also feeling a bit tentative about the fact that whoever caught me taking those photos won't be too thrilled to have come up empty-handed with only an empty flash memory card. Maybe he's figured out that I could have squirreled away more pictures. Make that singular—but at least that one image is safe on disk and in print.

Now I'm hungry for breakfast, and I order pancakes to go with the coffee I've been swilling. Anything's better than the ship's breakfast with choices like powdered eggs or scraggly toast with *whipped* butter, meaning half foamy air to stretch the margarine. I guess we're lucky, though—at least the butter's not done in fluorescent colors. I'll keep that to myself—the chef might jump at it. I'm sitting by the window where I can watch the ever-present rain slam against the glass. I've run out of reading matter, so I open my purse to get some of the ship's mail, which was slipped under our doors last night.

Oh, goodie—just what I needed—an invitation to a

private party in the captain's quarters, with a note from
the great Horatio himself:

Dear Ruby,
* It's my pleasure to invite you to attend an intimate*
gathering tonight not open to the public.

Uh-oh. I'll bet it'll be intimate, and I don't even want
to think about who's supposed to make it that way. Not on
your life, pal.

But I'm wrong. There's more:

* Guess what—this will be your chance to see my*
masculine lair—ha. I'm inviting only the Marquezes,
your rabbi, and, of course, my cousin Essie Sue and her
husband, Hal.

Okay. If this is legit, I think I'll go. I really like Sara
Marquez, and I'd like to know more about her husband,
Jack, too. And with Kevin invited, I won't be stuck with
Horatio as my date.

22

I know I'm in trouble as soon as I hit the door of the captain's quarters—it's way too quiet in here. And I hear faint dentist office music—a lethal combination when you're dealing with the Oily One. The light's so dim I can't see my hands in front of me, much less, I'm afraid, someone else's hands. I jump when a white-uniformed steward informs me that the captain will be joining me shortly, and that I should sit down. Is he kidding?

"Where did you come from?" I ask him, standing my ground and keeping an eye on the door. "Have you been here all along?"

"No, ma'am, you just didn't see me in the low light. Can I get you anything?"

"You can get me more light, please."

"I meant do you prefer a drink or something?"

"I meant that I prefer more light."

"I would, ma'am, but captain's orders are that we create an intimate atmosphere."

"Would that be the royal *we*, like you and the captain? Or the *we* that includes myself in the intimacy? Because if *we* don't get more light in here immediately, my part of the equation is walking right out the door."

"But Captain Goldberg has given strict orders—"

"You can tell your captain—"

"Ruby! How charming you look."

"How can you tell? I can't see a thing in here."

Horatio has outdone himself—he's sheathed in some sort of white sling full of medals and combat ribbons—I can imagine what kind of combat. I haven't seen so many badges since I was a Girl Scout. And he's sloshed himself with cologne. If he were emitting decibels instead of odors, he'd be screaming at me. As it is, I'm literally being knocked off my feet by the scent.

"How about one of our delicious cocktails, Ruby— mood-makers, I call them—you'll love it."

"The mood's already about as thick in here as the darkest movie theater—first let there be light, then I'll think about drinking."

He waves the steward toward the lights and I can finally see around me. The "quarters" definitely lean toward lair-ishness—lots of black leather and furry floor pillows. There's a plush leopard-skin-print sofa that I'm being edged toward, but—so far—successfully avoiding.

"You're not going to stand up the whole time you're here, are you?" Horatio is turning peevish.

"Well, maybe—as long as I'm the only one showing up. I thought you said six o'clock."

"For you, six, for everyone else, seven. Just a wee hour to get to know you—an hour is certainly in good taste— I'm nothing if not subtle, Ruby."

Well, he's not subtle, and the rest is obvious. I find an isolated chair with no arms and sit down.

"We make wonderful island cocktails in various colors—how about it?"

"No thanks, I'm kind of OD'd on the multicolored food. Do you have any of that guavaberry liqueur brought over from St. Martin? In the bottle so I can pour my own?"

I don't trust any potential mickeys concocted by the captain's hand, and this liqueur is fabulous. It's grown and made only a short distance away, so I'm sure he has it on board.

"A bottle of guavaberry for the lady, and Scotch for me."

Ha—even *he* doesn't go for the Technicolor tropical drinks. I expected some static about my choice, but now I realize he's hopeful I'll swill down a lot of the bottle. Not that it's easy to drink much liqueur, but if I do have more, it'll be after the others arrive.

"A toast to getting to know you, Ruby." That leer is positively revolting. "Your drink is normally an after-dinner treat, so I'll have more on hand later in the evening."

Yeah, I know it's an after-dinner drink, but since I no longer eat the dinners, I figure I can indulge myself. A handful of peanuts and a cup of coffee, and I'm all set for the night. I'll pass on any cute hors d'oeuvres and hope that there's not much they can do to alter the nuts. As for later in the evening, we won't go there. Ever.

"The ladies are usually impressed by my many emblems from sailing all over the world. Would you like to see them up close and personal?"

He leans over my little chair—fortunately, the Scotch has deodorized his breath somewhat—I never thought I'd be grateful for a whiff of alcohol up my nose, but considering the alternative, I'll take it. I'm more worried about the *personal* at the moment than the *up close*. He's shoving a chest full of medals at me, and is coming alarmingly near my face. This is obviously a well-practiced ploy, though I can't believe it might have ever worked. I stand up fast.

"Did Essie Sue know you were inviting me early?"

"Yes, she did—she thought it would be an excellent way for us to get acquainted, even though it's just a prelude to tonight. Tell me about yourself, Ruby."

With that, he holds his arms out—drink still in one hand—and goes for it. I'd die before I'd let him wrap himself around me, so I almost reflexively stomp on his foot and jump out of the way. As he grabs for his toe, the drink goes first, making a tannish stain on his white pants and all over his sheath of medals. He's lucky I went for his foot—I could have gone for his knee or worse.

With perfect timing, Kevin walks in.

"You're a half hour early," I say, recovering.

"I like to be early. What's the matter with the captain?"

"He spilled his drink."

Horatio's still hopping around holding his shoe and glaring at me. The steward is nervously dabbing at him with a napkin.

"I think your captain might need a change of uniform," I whisper to him, and tell Kevin we ought to give them some privacy.

"But I was invited to a cocktail party," he says.

"Maybe we should have our drinks out on deck," I say.

"No."

Uh-oh—Horatio's heard me.

"I'll be changed soon. The party goes on."

I decide to stay. First, I have to live onboard with this captain, slimy as he is. And besides, I'm not about to appear to be banished from the kingdom—he brought this on himself. Let him whine to his cousin Essie Sue—she'll believe whatever he tells her.

Before the captain comes back from his wardrobe change, Sara and Jack arrive. I notice that Essie Sue, usually never one to miss a minute, is noticeably late—I'm sure that was by mutual arrangement. Won't *she* be surprised.

Sara and I settle into a corner for a visit. We sit on the now safe leopard-skin couch, which is beyond comfortable. Wish I had it in my cabin instead of the board. Maybe I was wrong—Horatio probably attracted the women of the ship with this asset alone—especially the ones with bad backs.

Before we can even start to yak, Essie Sue arrives. I can tell she's disoriented, with the party in full swing without Horatio. She looks around and stares at me from the doorway. Sara notices and raises an eyebrow.

"I'll fill you in as soon as I can," I tell Sara. "You won't believe what just went on here."

"Can't wait," she says. It's nice to at least imagine having an ally—I'm so used to being the odd woman out in this crowd.

Essie Sue comes over and stands directly above us. "Where's my cousin, Ruby?"

"Why me? I don't keep up with his activities."

"Because you were the last one with him."

"And how would you know that? Maybe because you thought up the little pre–cocktail party tête-à-tête at six o'clock?"

Ha—I've caught her. Let's see her get out of it.

"I don't know what you're talking about."

"Fine. Why don't you go find Horatio and ask him?"

Right on cue, the captain appears in a new set of dress whites. The whole uniform shtick is so much a part of his identity that I wouldn't be surprised if he had half a dozen outfits as backup. But no medals—I guess he never figured on having them doused with alcohol. He looks a bit disoriented himself, and orders a double Scotch from the steward. Yep—he must have extra uniforms if he's willing to take a chance on Scotch again.

"I'd like some wine, Horatio. Where were you?"

"Changing my clothing, Essie Sue." He turns his back to our sofa, which is fine with me, since I'm not ready for more confrontations.

"You look peculiar, Horatio. Did Ruby take advantage of you?"

At this point, Sara cracks up.

"Think nothing of it," I whisper to her. "Blaming Ruby is blood sport with her—she's got it down to a fine point."

Essie Sue hustles Horatio off into a corner, and Sara turns to me.

"Okay, no more excuses. I want to hear details."

"My invitation to the party said six o'clock—I'm betting the captain and Essie Sue set it up. He told me it was to get better acquainted."

"Uh-oh. Don't stop here."

"He came on with a full-court press and I—well, reacted."

"You mean, just like that? With no warning?"

"I think he was counting on the element of surprise. Foreplay would have done him no good—I'd have had a chance to think about it and split. As it was, he ended up with a sore foot, stained trousers, and Scotch all over his collection of merit badges."

"I'd give anything to have been a fly on the wall—he's such a pompous man."

"I suppose he's capable of making my voyage even more miserable before it's over, so I'll just have to keep some distance between us."

"You can take refuge with us. Can I tell Jack?"

"Of course. The whole ship will know in a matter of minutes, anyway."

Essie Sue is still in the corner with Horatio, but she's facing me now and shaking her head.

"I'm ready to get out of here, Sara."

"Hey, don't leave *me* here in the loony bin. Jack and I found a tiny little bar tucked away on one of the upper decks—I'll tell him we'll be there."

I slip out the door and Sara follows. We head up the stairwell to the other deck.

"Is it indoors or out? It's actually stopped raining."

"It's in, but we can move outside if it stops for sure. Maybe the waiter can mop up a couple of chaises for us."

I'm so excited at the prospect of a relatively dry evening that I wait outside while Sara orders guavaberry drinks for us. The waiter obliges and we find ourselves plopped on the dry lounges before we know it.

"That can't be a half moon coming out from those clouds. Look," she says.

It's not exactly a full view of anything I'd call a moon, but a whole flock of black clouds are suddenly illuminated from behind by what has to be moonlight. I'm awestruck.

"The clouds do seem to be clearing, Sara. If I finally get to the beach tomorrow, I'm ready to make myself forget this whole soggy mess and start from day one."

"I'm crossing my fingers."

Jack finds us, grabs a towel, and cleans up a chair for himself.

"So what's the word from the captain's quarters, Jack?"

"They all went to dinner. Want to join them?"

"*No.*" We both answer in the same breath.

"Well, then, we can go to the burger bar whenever we feel like it."

"Sounds perfect to me."

"Your rabbi did ask about you, Ruby. Wanted to know where you went, but you looked as though you needed some space, so I didn't say."

"Thanks—more than I can say."

"I've never been around a rabbi before, but Sara and I have attended a couple of his lectures since we've been on board. I must say I found them fascinating. I guess they're the dead man's research, though, not his."

"Kevin just lucked into the laptop—he'd been holding it when the professor went down. I think he's done a pretty good job of getting out the information, though."

Sara raises another eyebrow. "With a little help from his friends, yes?"

"Yes—the best friend of all accidentally being the poor professor, of course."

I'm in such a relaxed mood that I almost start talking about some of the things Kevin and I found in the computer files, but at the last minute, I hold back. I'm suddenly remembering the list of names from El Paso, and that Jack and Sara Marquez were on that list. I honestly don't know how to approach this. Their interest in the Conversos rings true to me—just ordinary intellectual curiosity about an unusual subject. I can't assume any prior acquaintance with Gonzales on their part, and they've certainly never mentioned it. On the other hand, I'm frustrated. Like my dealings with Ed Levinger, though on a lesser scale here, I'm thinking I can go so far and no farther until I know more. And I won't know more until I'm able to ask more questions.

"Professor Gonzales made some prior sailings in these waters. You didn't happen to know him or know of him, did you?"

I'm mellowed out, but still sharp enough to be surprised by a quick look between them—one of those practiced looks between spouses that isn't even a look—just a flicker, no turn of the head being necessary.

"No," Jack says. They both shake their heads with no hesitation at all—not a wasted motion. I can't imagine I even let that question slip out, but now that it's done, it seems innocent enough.

"Me, either," I say. "I just met him at the raffle drawing, when Essie Sue introduced him to the crowd."

"Anybody for hamburgers?" Sara asks.

It seems a bit soon to break the spell the moonlight is casting, but we've skipped dinner, so they certainly have a reason to be hungry. I take one more look over the railing to see the diffused light shimmering over the water.

"I'm almost afraid to say it, guys, but do you realize we've had a whole hour without rain? That's a record for the trip."

We cross our fingers for tomorrow.

*

23

Magens Bay, on the north side of the island, is everything you'd want a Caribbean beach to be—the sand is white and the views of the Atlantic are breathtaking. Not that a glass of water in a sandbox wouldn't look good to me today, as long as the sun was shining on it. This is the first time I've even had a glimpse of blue waters. Our ship is docked on the Caribbean side of St. Thomas—the south side—and our bus has brought us across the island to the Atlantic side. I can tell it rains a lot here, because the plant life is even more opulent. But today it's gorgeous.

I've staked out a beach chair by Jack and Sara, figuring that if Essie Sue heads over here she'll be less likely to flip her lid in their genteel—make that *gentile*—presence. I'm sure she's gunning for me today after an earful last night from the would-be Lothario, Captain Goldberg. Jack's in the water already, and we've promised to join him when we get hot enough. For the moment, we're slathered with high-end sunblock in anticipation of the worst, and I'm being the tiniest bit intrusive.

"What's it like to be a banker's wife? Do people ever seek you out socially and then hit you up for mortgages when you least expect it?"

Sara fortunately notices that this is a joke, unlike some on this tour who choose not to get my rather bizarre sense of humor.

"Oh, sure—we have plenty of those. Bankers lead extremely busy social lives, as a matter of fact, and I, at least, harbor no illusions that our sparkling personalities are the attraction."

"You mean Jack does?"

"Let's just say he gets off on it more than I do. I'm athletic and I like to play golf, but it's Jack who likes the country club—the opposite of most couples in our circle, where the wives are the ones caught up in the club life."

"Have your families been on the border for a long time?"

"I'm from New Mexico myself—I grew up in Santa Fe. But Jack's family has lived on the Texas border for ages, back to when it was a part of Mexico. His grandparents spent their lives in a rural village in northern

Mexico, and he's quite proud that he was the first in his family to attend college. He's a pretty good businessman, too."

"I would imagine. How did he get his start?"

"Today we'd call it networking. He made some good friends at the university, and they didn't forget him when they were developing El Paso's downtown years ago. My family had some money, and we put in our share, too. He's made the most of it, and no one's been disappointed. He likes to say that he's a good family man, a devout Catholic, and a well-known Texas citizen."

"And you?"

"A little stifled by it all, but that's really nothing new. I was a restless child, too, and my own father wasn't that different from Jack. I married him, I guess."

"A lot of women do. But I wouldn't call a trip like this breaking away from it all—don't you have space that's just yours?"

"I've become interested in genealogy—the Web, of course, makes it much easier and also more exciting. That's my space, as you call it, and it's all mine because Jack's not interested. I like the fact that it's my project, but I wish sometimes that he'd want to trace his family— it would be great for our kids to have the information from both sides. I've learned a lot that I could teach him."

"Ha—maybe that's just what he doesn't want."

"That thought has occurred to me. And I know the kids can do it themselves if they're interested later. But still."

We see Jack waving from the surf, dripping and grinning as he comes in. We're *all* in a good mood from this break in the weather.

Sara leans toward me. "Ruby, I'd love to talk to you sometime about my own family roots. For a while there, I almost thought I had discovered a most peculiar Jewish heritage. I've since found out that this wasn't the case, but while I was in the midst of this obsession, I met people who shared some fascinating tales. That's why I've been so interested in your rabbi's lectures."

I can tell from her hurry that she doesn't want this to be a three-way conversation.

"Any time, Sara—I'd love it."

You can say that again. And I didn't even have to pry that hard.

Jack flops down beside us. "You two are chickens—haven't even dipped a toe yet. I thought you were going to join me."

"We were," I say, "but we got involved in an interesting conversation about Sara's genealogy."

"Oh, that." Jack gives out a groan. "I'm on vacation, Ruby, and I have to hear enough about what she finds on that computer when I'm at home. Not now—*please.*"

Oy—Sara's glaring at me. I certainly had no intention of mentioning the last part of her conversation with me, but I thought she specifically said she wished Jack were more interested in exploring genealogy with her.

"Sure," I say, "I'm all for R and R, and you're right—we haven't gotten our tootsies wet yet. How about it, Sara?"

"Just for a few minutes—then I'll come back and put some more sunblock on Jack—you need it, babe."

As soon as we wade in, I make my apologies.

"Hey, I knew you didn't want to talk about your family, but I guess I didn't realize the whole topic was off-limits. I thought maybe I could get him talking about *his* roots and spark some interest for you."

"I realized that as soon as you got the words out, but I was just worried at first that you might spill the rest of it inadvertently."

"Trust me, the subject is off the table until next time you want to talk about it. Isn't the water great?"

The rain has lowered the water temperature, but I love it just the same—it's invigorating. A few squeals and we're used to it. I want to run out a ways and ride back in on the bigger waves, but Sara seems timid.

"I just want to get wet and feel the sea," she says, "then I'm ready to go back to the beach. This is my chance to see Jack without all the business competition."

"Yeah, I know the feeling—my husband tried to get away, but we seldom had vacation time just for ourselves. Grab all you can get."

Sara slogs through the surf to shore, and I go farther out. A big breaker comes up and almost knocks me down, but I jump from the shifting sand beneath me and ride with it. If I go out even more, I'll be able to float and really take advantage of the lift of the waves—there's much less risk of being knocked down when you're in deeper water.

It's amazing to me how many women don't enjoy the

ocean—maybe they're afraid of the loss of control that comes with letting yourself be carried away by the tide. And then, of course, there's that whole category of hairdo freaks who don't like the rough water because it messes them up. And in punishment for my blasphemous thoughts, the prime example of that type, Essie Sue, wearing a honey-colored satin suit matching her hair perfectly, waves frantically from the shore. She's wading ankle-deep in the surf—which tells me right off that she's a tad anxious to get to me. This woman does not, and I repeat *not,* expose even her toenail polish to the risks of the briny deep unless she has to.

She might well want to see me, but I don't have to reciprocate. In fact, I'm inhabiting the best of all possible water worlds out here—I'm safe, floating easily in the salty Atlantic, and not in the least hurry to have my belated vacation day spoiled.

I'm also apparently cursed in some way, because whether she's willed it or not, and I suspect she has—a huge wave washes in, picks me up, and virtually carries me to shore, depositing me dripping and sputtering at her feet. Yes, the woman has power—the source of which I wouldn't want to bet on.

"Good, Ruby—you're here."

An understatement if ever I heard one.

"We need to talk. Do you even vaguely realize how hurtful and disrespectful you've been to my cousin Horatio? The man's a leader among men—an honored international naval officer with underlings catering to his every whim, and you dare to pour a drink on him? He opens his home to you, and you embarrass him at his own soiree?"

I'm barely standing, my eyes burning from the salt-water, and half dizzy from being slammed into the sand.

"Say what?" Fortunately, there's liquid in my ears. I wouldn't want to have to hear quite everything she's yelling, though I do get the gist.

She crosses the line when she takes my hand and pulls me a few inches away from the water. Anything to keep her toenail polish from chemically disintegrating.

"I can kick sand in your face from this position, Essie Sue. So quit screaming at me."

"I want an explanation."

"Not that I owe you one, but since I'm sure you've inflamed the whole ship by now, just listen. I'm only say-ing this once. Your cousin is a letch. He came after me with both arms open, ready to grab me and lock those tentacles around my body. I stepped on his toe hard, and he dropped his own drink all over those showy medals of his. This was in addition to the fact that he invited me there alone under false pretenses, which you know very well and probably instigated. End of story."

"That's not what he told me. He was being a gracious host, stepped over to ask you out on a date—which in my opinion you ought to be grateful for—and before he could say anything, you kicked him and threw a drink all over his beautiful uniform. What do you have to say for yourself?"

"I told you I wasn't repeating this. Get lost, and tell him to stay away from me."

Just as I turn from her and go back in the sand toward Jack and Sara, a genuine miracle occurs. A breaker, much more gigantic than the one that brought me to shore, rises from the deep and hurls toward the spot where Essie Sue's still venting. It knocks her down, and yes, it's not just the toenails this time—her hairdo comes into full contact with the saline solution. In other words, she's soaked.

There is a sea god, after all.

24

It's the first evening that hasn't been preceded by a day of rain—not such a startling fact until you consider what it means—all the decks are dry. If they weren't, of course, I'd be a valuable commodity because my sunburned body alone could radiate enough dry heat to suck the moisture from the wood beneath me. I was so busy watching Sara slathering Jack with lotion that I forgot to renew my own—I thought one application early in the morning would be enough. It wasn't, and every inch of me is paying for the miscalculation. Avoiding both Essie Sue and the captain is taking more energy than I care to expend, and the result is that I'm feeling sorry for myself.

On the other hand, I'm so grateful for the beautiful evening that I want to celebrate. This is "nothing" night, thank heavens—not Las Vegas Night, or Seafarer's Night, or the big costume ball everyone's preparing for—even the meal downstairs was in blessed monochrome. The fish was left alone, the bread wasn't dyed some awful aqua in honor of the sea, and we had plain mashed potatoes. I was definitely in the mood for comfort food. I changed clothes, and now I'm dressed in comfort colors—a light blue shirt in the softest cotton I could find, and white shorts with sandals.

Lots of people showed up for dinner. Since the ship isn't lurching anymore, the seasickness quotient has obviously dropped considerably.

I'm looking over the rail at the exact place where I met Ed the other night, with half of me terrified he'll show up here again and the other half hoping that he might. Talk about being of two minds—picking my way through the crummy events of the last few days would be so much easier with his help. If only I trusted him. And vice versa, I guess.

As if he'd read my mind, he appears in that noiseless way of his and fits in as though he'd been here for the last hour. He smells of suntan lotion this time, and it turns out we're almost look-alikes—sandals, white denim shorts, and a pale, narrow-blue-striped shirt he's wearing. Together we make me think of those Hawaiian shirt couples in Honolulu. Ed's clothes always look comfortable on him in that casual way guys without the same build or attitude would kill for. My own cerebral Stu looked like a long, thin drink of water in his extra-longs, and men like Kevin unfortunately can't wear anything without calling up visions of an alteration person kneeling down in front of them with a mouth full of pins.

Ed's pushing that same brown lock out of his eyes all the time so I know he's not exactly at ease, but that's the only uneasiness that shows.

"Hi."

Oy. I even like his *His.* Assured, but very *un*-meet and greet. He'd make a lousy politician. Except, of course, women would get it right away.

"Want to hang out for a while tonight, Ruby?"

"You know, I'm not exactly sure."

"Yeah. I do know."

I look at him long enough to see that he's as regretful as I am, and no more certain of what to do about it.

"Look, Ruby, before you run out on me again, or we get interrupted by one of the Obnoxious Ones, let's work out a truce for now. I really like it when you're dancing with me and not around me."

"It's all about me, huh?"

"No—I've been edging around you, too. And possibly we'll decide to do something about that, but could we not do it tonight? If we spend some real time together, maybe we'll know what to do."

"Okay. You've got a point. I feel *up* today with that interminable rain out of the way, and we are on a cruise."

"Of sorts."

We both laugh, and not a moment too soon. Essie Sue and her husband, Hal, are passing the only part of the deck above that's visible from here. If we can see them, they can see us, and undoubtedly will. Ed takes my hand and we make a run for it.

"They don't deserve to find our private view," he says. "They'd just preempt it."

"No, they'd stake us out to see what we were doing. This way, they'll never know we were there. Where are we headed?"

"Trust me for a minute, Rothman. I know just the place."

We go down one deck and in back of the casino area.

"Oh no—not the karaoke room. I have visions of the captain mouthing the words to 'You're My Everything.'"

"Don't jump to conclusions. But yeah, I heard about the foiled seduction—it's all over the ship."

"Thanks. I really needed to hear that."

"Guess I'd better keep in shape in case he challenges me to a duel over you."

"Ha. He wants nothing to do with me—you're safe on that one."

"So whaddaya think?"

I look around me at the mercifully small-scale room with hard floor space in front of the carpeting for the performers.

"Well, at least it's not pink and gigantic. But it's the karaoke room."

"Not for tonight it isn't—nothing's scheduled. And

they've got a ton of CDs—some of them oldies. With the door closed, the place is ours."

"If Horatio said that, I'd run for the hills."

"There are more things in heaven and earth, Horatio, than are dreamt of under your toupee."

I'm shrieking. "You've got to be kidding—that blond hair is a rug? I thought it was just peroxide."

"If you'd stayed longer and hadn't kicked the guy in the medals, you'd have known."

"Funny, Levinger. And I didn't kick him. I stomped him."

"Whatever—I'm wearing my athletic equipment, just in case."

He picks out a CD and shows it to me.

I'm amazed. "'Star Dust' and 'Deep Purple,' too? I can't believe they have these."

He pulls me onto the stage area we're using as a dance floor, and stops talking.

It's that great fit I remember from the last time we danced, or almost danced. We didn't even finish one song that night before something revolting happened—I don't even remember what at the moment, and I don't want to—this is too nice to spoil.

He dances in the same unruffled way he moves when he's off the dance floor—nothing fancy, but who wants fancy? He has the touch I like, and I must say, the way he holds me shows great promise. Maybe I have a short memory, but "Star Dust" never sounded this good.

I'm not sure when the holding turned from dancing to

a kiss, but it sure sneaked up on me with the slightest turn of the head. And it answers one question—I don't have to wonder now if he likes this. It's amazing to me how many men kiss only because they know women love it. They cultivate the whole megillah, but they're not into it. And, boy, can a woman tell the difference. I've met super machos, extremely uptight in the *he-ness* department, who just can't bend to it—you can tell they're put off, but feel they're expected to hurry through anyhow.

Hurry being the operative word. Ed doesn't hurry through anything, and this, he obviously enjoys as much as I do. He's very deliberate, very sexy. And he has lots and lots of patience.

Talk about harbingers.

25

E-mail from: Ruby
To: Nan
Subject: *Fun and Games—I Think*

I'm engaged in a serious mind-body con-
flict. Ed and I spent a long time dancing
in our karaoke hideaway last night,
interrupted only when one of the Elvis
look-alikes dropped in to practice for
tomorrow night's contest. But I certainly
can't say we'd been rushed. Of course,
switching to the other meaning of the
word, *I've* been rushed like a sorority
girl—that's part of the problem. If I'd

said, *Whoa, Ruby,* to myself one more time last night, you could have fed me oats.

It's obvious that we're both having a good time together, which would be simple if it weren't for the multitasking going on underneath the program. This could be a fun shipboard romance, but it's undercut by all the unanswered questions we have about one another.

See if you can hurry along Paul Lundy's query into the handling of Professor Gonzales's body—that could tell us a lot. Although if there's foul play there, I still won't know how Ed might or might not be connected with it, will I? Do you think I should confide in him? My instinct tells me he's kosher in all this, but how do I know my hormones aren't influencing my gut? It wouldn't be the first time.

I've slipped down to the café this morning because I'm really feeling in need of your take on things and wanted to get this e-mail out. I have my bathing suit on under my shorts. As soon as I get back to the dock we're off for an excursion to Buck Island, a diving area with a remote feel to it even though it's not that far from Charlotte Amalie. Ed wasn't signed up for it but might try to be included at the last minute—hope there's room for him. Of course Essie Sue had our group registered for this outing before the Year One, so we'll all be gathered en masse.

We'll be sailing to the island on a yacht—wish you were with us. Buck Island is uninhabited—it's a national marine park, and I hear we'll be anchoring in a protected cove for snorkeling. We'll see how many from Temple Rita get their hair wet!

26

The sky is overcast, but at least there's no rain. I'm pysched—outside of my fantasies, I've never been aboard a yacht. I understand champagne is usually the order of the day, but I hear Essie Sue's arranged for root beer instead—yuck. Her only reason was "I know this crowd—no one's up for champagne." Or it just might be that her cousin has instigated yet another "cost-cutting measure" and she doesn't want to publicize it.

I'm a little late arriving at the dock, but nothing's happening anyway.

Essie Sue's done up in her nautical navy from Neiman's for the trip—topped with a little sailor hat that looks like it came from a toy store.

"You're late, Ruby. Why didn't you meet after breakfast like I suggested?"

Make that *ordered,* but who cares. "Couldn't make it.
Where's the yacht?"

"See, if you'd shown up for the orientation, you'd
have known the answer to that question. The yacht was
tied up."

Duh.

"The yacht was otherwise engaged, and there was a
mix-up. So we're sailing on one of the motor barges."

"You know, Essie Sue, I'm very appreciative of my sta-
tus as a lottery winner, but aren't you getting some flack
from the others about all these substitutions? After all,
they paid for a yacht and they're getting—"

Oy . . . what they're getting is just pulling up. It smells
like an oil barge, but it's flying our ship's flag. And I don't
want to say it's slow but I'm calculating that it'll reach
nearby Buck Island by midnight. I could swim faster. But
she was right about one thing—root beer is the appropriate toast of the day. I'll bet anything she's known this for
a while.

"Let me worry about the others, Ruby. I'm having to
cover my head with this sailor hat the rabbi lent me, all
because of the ocean dunking you were responsible for
the other day. The saltwater gave my hair a greenish cast,
and even the ship's beauty salon couldn't fix it. See?"

She takes off the sailor hat—not exactly Kevin's style,
either—and makes me peer into the strands on her head.
I don't see anything.

"It looks like normal to me."

"No, it's green. Green-*ish*."

"It looks fine."

"That's what the beauty operator said, but what does she know?"

"Okay, it's green. Maybe you should have worn green instead of navy."

Before she tells me why she wore navy, I look around for Ed, but don't see him. Maybe he caught wind of the barge change.

"All aboard, people. The rabbi's with us, so I'm sure we'll have good weather and good sailing."

Uh-huh. In my experience, Kevin seems to bring on disaster, not ward it off. I always hated that kind of superstition foisted on the clergy. I wish I had a dime for every time someone said something like that to Stu or even, heaven forbid, to me. People were especially happy boarding airplanes with us, I remember—they thought it would make the flight crashproof. Which was pretty funny since Stu had to take a Valium every time he flew.

And on the flip side, of course, they wanted us to do a disappearing act whenever some suspected naughtiness was about to come up—as if we'd never seen anyone drunk, stoned, or scantily clad: *You'd better leave, Rabbi— so-and-so would be terribly embarrassed if he thought you were here seeing him this way.*

I'm glad I had some breakfast at the café before "setting sail," as they say, although to use those words anywhere near this clunker of a boat is laughable. If I hadn't eaten, I'd really feel queasy—the thing is emitting black fumes that smell like burning tires. I wander over to the side to see if I can find the ladder or an opening in the rail where we'll descend for our snorkeling, but nothing's there. It's obvious that this is no sight-seeing vessel. We'll all have to climb the rails and jump overboard to snorkel, which is really gonna go over with this crowd. It's fine with me, though—I'd walk the plank to get off this dinghy.

We chug our way across the water toward Buck Island. Essie Sue suggests a round of seafarer's songs, but the crowd wisely declines, and she doesn't insist. Maybe she's slightly overcome herself.

"Rabbi, why don't you give a blessing for the voyage?"

Oy, she hasn't given up on that yet. I see Sara Marquez's eyebrows go up. She and Jack have obviously wrangled tickets—I wish Ed had.

"Come on, Essie Sue." Maybe Brother Copeland will bring her to her senses. "The rabbi's dressed for swimming, not praying."

"For your information, Brother, you don't have to be dressed to pray. How about it, Rabbi?"

Kevin, fashionable in his plaid bathing trunks and a striped tee shirt, looks from one to the other, and obviously decides it's safe to take on Essie Sue as long as Brother's here.

"I don't know any voyager prayers—you didn't tell me I'd have to prepare."

Brother pats him on the back. "See? Let the man have some time off."

Essie Sue doesn't look ready to let anyone off, so I change the subject and hope she'll forget about it. "Kevin, I hope you brought along a spare shirt."

"No, I'm going to strip this one off and leave it on the boat."

"You could get a real burn on your back if you're in the water for a long time—maybe you can borrow a shirt."

"I'll be underwater the whole time, Ruby—remember?"

"Uh—Kevin, I don't think you understand about snorkeling. What do you think you'll be doing?"

"I'm gonna wear some kind of air mask and go down to the bottom. They're going to show us how."

"No, snorkeling's done from the surface. You wear a pair of goggles and breathe through a tube. You just float along and watch the fish beneath. At least, I hope you can watch them—with this half-murky water, who knows?"

"No, Ruby, I know I'm going underwater—the brochure said so."

"That's scuba diving, Kevin. Where you get all decked out in a rubber suit and carry a tank on your back. That enables you to descend all the way to the bottom."

"Yep. That's what we paid for."

"Do you have a dive certificate?"

"A what?"

"I didn't think so. Diving's a whole other sport— much more complicated and requiring lessons from a qualified instructor. You can't just put the outfit on and dive."

"Essie Sue'll take care of it. You're always a spoilsport, Ruby."

Not even Essie Sue can perform that miracle, but if that's what he wants to think, let him. And I even tried to get him off the hook.

We're finally pulling up close to the island. I want to be one of the first off so I don't have to be involved with teaching these people to put on masks and flippers— that's what the staff is paid for. If I don't disappear fast, Essie Sue will have me instructing. I perch on the side of the barge and wait until they say we can get in the water.

To my surprise, almost everyone wants to go snorkeling—they're either light-headed from the emissions or the aversion to staying around this burning oil is universal. At any rate, even the older people are standing in line ready to be hoisted over the rails and down to the water, which is unfortunately not blue, but olive green under today's cloudy skies. It's translucent if not transparent, but at least you can partially view the depths. Which is the point, of course—I hope the visibility is better once I'm a few inches underwater.

I'm the first to jump down, and I'm surprised the water's so cold—maybe I'm just not used to it. I decide to swim before slipping my equipment on—putting some distance between myself and the others, and looking for a nice natural cove to be my headquarters. The island's rocky, and I have no desire at the moment to climb up and explore it—I'd rather see what fish I can find underneath. The group's nearby, and I can hear squeals as everyone hits the cold water.

I find a protected area and climb up on a low-hanging rock. It's good to get away from the rest of the crowd— the trip over here on the crowded barge was about as much as I could take. I'd love to be snorkeling with Ed. He knows so many people down here, I'm wondering if he could still show up on another boat—he might even be lucky enough to hitch a ride on a catamaran and sail over.

Wishful thinking, Ruby. I should just be glad it's not pouring.

I'm excited about the variety of sea life visible in these waters—sea turtles, parrot fish, angelfish, yellowtail snapper, and all kinds of coral, tube sponges, and anemones. The sun's going in and out—better than the overcast skies earlier, and I'm hoping I can see something. I already have my fins on, so I add the mask and snorkel and float out from the cove. Nothing at first except murky depths, but then the sun illuminates a little section of the water and I can see the coral beneath—big boulder coral and those neat tube sponges that look like cutoff pipes. And finally fish! There's a whole school of yellowtail snapper swimming by down below, and I can clearly see a wide yellow stripe running down the side of each fish and turning into a V as it hits the tail.

I'm dying to try scuba diving—there's a whole world

straight down from here that I'd like to explore. Swimming has always been a meditative experience for me—when I'm doing lap swims, I space out into a reverie that's totally removed from this life. I can't imagine what it would be like to go down ninety or a hundred feet and experience the underwater gardens filled with waving tendrils and giant sponges.

The stress is leaving my body as I float almost in a trancelike state, moving my flippers in an arc as I curve around the cove. I use one hand to swat the back of my neck where some large insect must have landed, and kick slowly on to the next spot. I feel that faint flickering on my neck again—it's vaguely annoying, and I try to submerge a few more inches. I don't know how many seconds pass before I realize that what's on my neck is not ethereal—it's quite heavy. It takes a few more seconds for me to understand that the force on the back of my neck is tactile and deliberate.

It's a hand.

I can feel the fingers tightening around my neck and pushing me straight down. For a minute I breathe through my snorkel tube, but as soon as I hear the *thwup* of the tube top submerging under the surface, I pull it off my face. I thrash reflexively and move my hands and legs like a spider under glass, but the hand presses harder and harder. I try to swerve around and see my attacker, but my head is held immobile. I dive lower, but the hand follows me. I relive the dizziness I felt as a child when we'd see who could hold a breath the longest. I become a child, held down during a tantrum, arms and legs flailing to no avail.

My mind fights with every command in its arsenal, but my body can't carry out the orders. Finally, I let the blackness in.

27

At the same time as I slip under, I hear a voice.

"Ruby, are you over here? Ruby?"

It's Kevin, and I come to life enough to see the foam in the water where he's kicking.

The hand leaves, and the back of my neck springs up as though a flatiron had been lifted from it. The new feeling of weightlessness and life is indescribable, but I'm too weak to take advantage of it. The darkness is taking over again, and I feel my head sliding back into the water. I can't believe my senses are so acute, but Kevin's voice is actually magnified. It sounds as though it's coming from an echo chamber:

"Ruby, I can't get my mask to work right—it's foggy, and the guy says he can't spend any more time on me. I've been searching for you for fifteen minutes."

He's not close enough to grab—I can just hear him in that totally surreal fashion. I guess it gradually dawns on him that I'm going down, and he calls out.

"Hey, I think Ruby's in trouble—help! I don't know how to save anybody!"

My head bobs up again and I strain every muscle to swim to the rock on shore, but it doesn't work—I just don't go anywhere. I turn on my back, breathing in the wonderful fresh air, rest for a minute. Then I try moving my legs and just flopping my flippers in a kind of back-stroke that points me toward shore. I combine that with a weak sidestroke that actually propels me forward in a choppy sort of way. The rock isn't that far from me now. It takes a superhuman effort to pull myself up, but I do it. Then I pass out.

I think I'm hallucinating when I see Ed in a pair of bathing trunks kneeling above me. The look of concern on his face scares me, but I'm coughing too much to say anything. He cradles my head in his arms and raises me to a half-sitting position. My throat and nasal passages are killing me, but I keep pointing at my mouth.

"What?" he says. "What do you want, honey? Do you want a drink?"

The last thing I want is more water. I swallow and then take a deep breath.

"Have to talk."

"Why don't you wait a minute until you can catch your breath?"

He's moved me around so that my back can rest on his chest. I shake my head and point at my mouth again.

"Okay, tell me in my ear," he says.

He bends his head down and I whisper, which is all I seem able to do. The words come out like they've been vibrating on an emery board instead of my vocal cords.

"Scared?" That's all I can get out on the first try.

"Who? You?"

I shake my head no and point at him.

"Yes," he says, "I am. You scared me."

"Am I okay?" I'm finding my voice now.

"You're fine now, Ruby."

"You looked as if I'd come back from the dead."

"You did. Your face was totally white when I got to you, and you weren't breathing."

"How?" I point to Kevin, who's standing a few feet away, surrounded, I see now, by a knot of people.

"Kevin called for help and I heard him. I'd just arrived—I hitched a ride with a friend of mine on his sailboat—I was going to surprise you."

"Kevin went to find you?"

"I swam over when I heard him say you were in trouble. And by the way, you're not being bothered by the rest of the pack because I commandeered this space as a no visitors zone—they were leaning in and crowding out all your air. I figured that'd be okay with you."

I nod.

"It's decidedly not okay with your friend Essie Sue—she's scowling at me as we speak."

I close my eyes and lie back. My mind isn't working too well, but a little reflex tells me I'd be enjoying this if my senses weren't defunct. As for Essie Sue, I can't even take that in—it's a nice feeling.

I open my eyes again and Ed tells me I passed out for a few minutes.

"Your breathing was fine, so I decided you just needed to drift off. I'm assuming you're not ready to move yet."

"I just want to sleep—I'm so tired." I try to shift positions, but my body feels like it's had six hours of aerobics, nonstop. "I'll never be able to get up and walk, Ed."

"Don't worry about it. This is a U.S. territory, remember—a Coast Guard cutter's bringing over a stretcher and some medics. Not that I couldn't carry you to the barge, but the cutter has a bed—you'll be much more comfortable."

"Oh no. I don't need that—just help me sit up." Suddenly, I want to come back to life. The word *stretcher* did it. Next thing I know, they'll be taking me to a hospital. I stay out of those when I can.

"Are you sure you want to sit on your own?"

"Yeah. Let's just see if I can keep my balance."

He helps me straighten up, and although the dizziness comes back for a second, I'm okay. This gesture seems to be a signal to the crowd, and they all swarm around me.

"Hey! Give her a chance!" Ed yells.

"It's all right. I'm better." I can see Sara and Jack are

concerned, but with enough common sense not to be in the way right now—they're standing back.

"Ruby, I called for help for you." Kevin's an inch away from my face.

"I think I remember hearing you, Kevin. Thanks."

"I would have given you artificial respiration, but I never took that course."

"I know—that's fine. Did I fight you when you got near me?"

"I didn't *get* near you—a person could die from that already. Everybody knows not to approach a drowning man."

"The rabbi saved your life, though," Essie Sue says, pushing him aside for the premier space two feet in front of me. "If he hadn't said you were in trouble, none of us would have known."

"But it was Levinger who found her on the rock." Mrs. Chernoff pats Ed on the back. "He might have even done CPU on you, Ruby." She's taking computer lessons at the senior center, but I get the point. Ed winks at me, and I'm so exhausted I can't even say anything appropriate. I just look at him.

"I didn't have to perform CPU," he says. "Ruby rescued herself."

I'm hoping that's true. I don't like those stories where your life suddenly belongs to someone who saved you— not even Ed.

I'm feeling relieved, but I'm not to be totally spared— Essie Sue never misses a good kick when I'm down.

"You should be ashamed of yourself for wandering so far off. And especially if you weren't a good swimmer."

"Lay off, Essie Sue." Ed gives her one of her own looks, and she shuts up.

We see the Coast Guard boat approaching, and the whole group goes in their direction to wave them in.

"I guess you provided some pretty exciting entertainment for your group," Ed says. "I've never seen them so animated." His voice is jovial but his eyes are still frightened.

"I'll be all right, I promise," I say. "And I'll be able to tell you—"

"If I hear the words *thank you* right now, I'm leaving—I didn't do anything. Your promising to be okay is all I want to hear. I mean it, Ruby—don't."

"You'll find me very pliable today."

"Well, that's a switch. I don't want to upset you, but now that you've come to, and since you-know-who isn't here to criticize, could you tell me what happened to pull you under? Did you get a cramp?"

I didn't know a person could seesaw between confusion and horror, but that's what I'm doing.

"Ed, don't you know?"

"Know what?"

"What pushed me down."

"What do you mean?"

"The hand. The person's hand. Didn't you see someone swimming away?" I hear my voice becoming shrill as

I realize the enormous assumptions I've made. I thought everyone *knew* what happened to me today. But then, I've been so groggy I'm not sure if I even remembered myself until now.

"You mean to tell me someone tried to drown you?"

All of a sudden, I'm wary. I'm afraid he'll think I'm hysterical.

"Ed, do you believe me?"

As if by some weird coincidence, I turn my head a bit too fast to look at him, and I'm hit with a stifling slam of pain in the back of my neck. I grab the spot with my hands and howl—or at least, that's what it sounds like to me. The group on the beach turns to look.

"This is how it was done," I say, trying to calm down. "Someone pushed my neck down in the water and tried to kill me."

He holds me tighter—reflexively, I think, then lets up. "Of course I believe you. But who would have any reason to kill you here in the islands? And how could he have disappeared so fast?"

"I'm sure the person swam away when Kevin called me—that's when the grip lightened on my neck and I surfaced. There are passengers here and lots of crew, too— it could have been someone connected with the ship, or a complete stranger."

My throat's hurting—I'm talking too much. And I'm suddenly remembering there are secrets I'm keeping about *somebody's* business, even though I don't know whose—things I haven't told Ed. Fortunately, I don't have to think about them right now, because two sailor-looking guys are headed toward me with a stretcher. The Coast Guard, no doubt. And guess what—even the idea of a stretcher isn't bothering me—I'm too exhausted to care.

28

The trip back to Charlotte Amalie is a blur—I'm fairly comfortable in a clean bunk bed and Ed's here—otherwise, I'm not taking in much. Essie Sue and Kevin have forced themselves on the Coast Guard—never let it be said that a branch of government was a fair match for these people.

As Essie Sue puts it, "This is faster than the boat we came over on, and less smelly, so why shouldn't they take us aboard?"

"I'm glad she said that," Ed says. "I wouldn't want anyone under the mistaken impression she's riding along out of concern for you."

"Please. There are people whose concern you *don't* want, and she heads the list."

"And as far as the rabbi's heroic rescue that he keeps bragging about, give me a break." Ed's pacing up and down the cramped aisle by my bed. "He wanted you to help him with something, as usual, and he didn't even try to drag you out of the water."

"Don't keep replaying it, hon. I made it." I motion for him to stop his pacing—it makes me dizzy. He sits on the foot rail of the bed.

Oy. These *hon*s are slipping out all over the place, and we really aren't that far along. Of course, how far along do you have to be when someone was prepared to save you from drowning? I'll work it out later—it's making me too anxious now. All I want to do is hold his hand and not think.

An ambulance picks us up at the docks and, with the siren silent, takes me sedately to the hospital. Ed, Essie Sue, and Kevin have to stay at the pier and talk to the police, who, having been called by the Coast Guard, are already waiting at the entrance to the ship. Mercifully, I'm supposedly sick enough to postpone my own interview until the doctor looks at me.

I thank the ambulance driver for not running red lights. As I expected, the emergency room doctor says I check out pretty good—I'm just bereft of any strength. She's pretty sure I won't have to stay the night, but I'm put into a temporary space that looks like an ordinary hospital room, complete with telephone, and I get to stretch out flat on the bed.

"Hey, can I use this phone for long distance?" I ask the attendant.

He tells me as long as I have a calling card, which I do. I've memorized it. I've got to call Nan at work, since who knows how long it'll be until I get back to that Internet café. She'll be crazy if she doesn't hear from me, and she's liable to call Paul Lundy in a panic. I don't want to bring in Paul until I talk with Ed—I don't need Paul pressuring me to fly home early. This nice private space is more calling room than I've had for the whole vacation, and all it costs me is the price of a credit card call. I'd also rather talk to Nan while Ed's not here.

I call her direct extension and she's there.

"Hi, babe—it's me, from St. Thomas." Hope I'm sufficiently jolly to alleviate any preliminary worries.

I'm not.

"What's the matter? You sound like a truck ran over you and you're calling from the operating room."

Close. This is what I get for having a friend who knows me too well. And who's probably psychic, to boot. I read in some Oprah book that you're never supposed to let anyone inside your head. It's obviously too late for that now.

"Well, as a matter of fact, I am waiting temporarily in a hospital room, but they're letting me go as soon as I get off the phone."

"You lie."

"No, really—I'm only using this bed to sit on because there are no chairs in here," I lie.

"Ruby, let me speak to the doctor, okay?"

"Look, I only have a few minutes to be by myself. Trust me and listen first—then I'll let you talk to whoever you want."

I try to explain fast, starting from early this morning until now. I give her the whole megillah, pulling no punches about the near-drowning incident, the would-be killer who got away, and Ed's finding me on the rock.

"But he doesn't know about the assault in the temple backyard, does he?"

"No, I was holding back because he held back with *me* about his erasing those laptop files. And his being with that man who had the briefcase. I need to figure out more about him."

"So have you figured out more?"

"No, but now I have more to factor in. I simply can't believe that a guy as sincerely concerned about me as he's been today could do me harm."

"So the real purpose of this call is to get my feedback on whether or not you should confide in Ed. Am I right?"

"In a way, I guess. I'm taking a big risk here with someone I've known for a very short time, and spent one romantic evening dancing with—period."

"It is risky, but if you're determined not to tell the police about the temple thing or the laptop, then how else are you going to learn anything *without* Ed? You ought to tell him for your own safety. We know he's a good investigative reporter, and in all fairness, he doesn't know a lot about you, either—why should he have confided in you earlier, any more than you in him? He might even be working with the police, for all you know."

"I just don't want to think my judgment's been suddenly clouded because of an attraction. That's why I need your take."

"Look, tell him right off about Paul Lundy's involvement—that could be insurance for you if you're wrong about him—he'll know the police were notified. My real point is that the sooner you confide in him, the sooner more people can be alerted for your protection."

I hear someone at the door.

"Gotta go."

"Do it, Ruby. And call me."

I manage to hang up the phone as the doorknob turns—it's Ed, back from the police questioning, but he's not alone. Essie Sue and Kevin are right behind him.

Essie Sue immediately perches on the bed. "I think Ruby should spend the night here."

"No."

"The rabbi thinks so, too."

"Yeah, Ruby, you still look sick."

"Thanks for your concern, Kevin, but I can get just as much rest in my cabin." I can't, really, but I just don't like hospitals.

"Ed, did you check with the emergency room doctor? She said I wouldn't have to spend the night."

"She said you could go if you're feeling better. I gather you are?"

"I'll feel better if this room isn't so crowded."

"Don't you want to hear about our police interrogation?" Essie Sue's practically on top of me.

"Yes, tell me."

"They asked all sorts of questions about you—whether you were feeling well or could have gone into water too deep for you. I believe they thought you might have been committing suicide."

"No such luck, Essie Sue. I intend to be around for a while."

I look at Ed, wondering if he told the police what really happened. He shakes his head no. *Oy.* Just what I need—another person reading my mind.

"I told them all about my rescue," Kevin says. "They congratulated me for it."

"That's great, Kevin. Now, when can I get out of here? Do I have to see the police today?"

"No, they know you're a cruise passenger and that you're not leaving for a few days. They'd like you to come down to the station tomorrow, though. Just routine, despite what Essie Sue said. It's not as though they've never had tourists go under before."

"Then why are they involved at all?"

"Because the Coast Guard patrol had to be called—it's protocol."

"I guess that's it for our wonderful day on Buck Island," Essie Sue says. "You gave us quite an ending."

"If I remember, Essie Sue, you were thrilled to ride back with the Coast Guard to get away from the wonderful smelly barge you arranged for us, with the root beer toasts."

"Okay, everybody out," Ed says. "Ruby's got to get ready to leave."

"You're going back with Ed?" Kevin says.

"Yep."

"Remember, Ruby—you have to think about your costume for the ball," Essie Sue says. "The captain is a forgiving man. He admits that there might have been a slight misunderstanding between you and him the other night, and he'd like to talk it over with you." She looks at Ed, then back at me. "So don't put all your eggs in one basket."

"How about me?" Kevin says. "I can use a date for the dance, too. I think the women on this ship are prejudiced against the clergy. One girl told me that whenever she sees me she feels like confessing."

"Don't knock it before you try it," Ed says.

Essie Sue's getting up from my bed. "Enough already, Rabbi—I can't fix everything. We'll see about Ruby if nothing else works out."

"Gee, I'm overwhelmed with the popularity. Where were all of you in junior high?"

Ed's biting his lip. "This is gonna be tough competition," he says to me. "But at least I make my own arrangements."

"Ha!" I say. "That's what you think—you just don't know the group dynamics yet."

We try to wipe the smiles off our faces as Essie Sue pulls Kevin out the door and the doctor comes in.

"Let's take a little spin around the room," she says, "and see how you hold up."

"I'll get up if you'll call it something different—*spin* is too close to reality, and I've experienced enough dizziness for one day."

I walk gingerly around my bed and then back and forth beneath the window. Everything's fine—I'm just tired, but I don't say anything more about that. Not that I'm dying to go back to my berth, but at this point, being on the ship seems that much closer to normality.

"Keep in touch with your infirmary," the doctor says, "and tell them to call the hospital if anything changes for the worse—not that I think it will. You've just been through a trauma, that's all, and there may be aftershocks. Be on your guard."

29

We ride back to port in a taxi, not saying much—Ed's probably as exhausted as I am. I'm glad he's not asking questions because I have a lot to work out in my mind. I'm about ready to tell him everything, assuming he reciprocates, but I don't feel quite up to negotiating yet. We pull up at the dock and head for my cabin area on the bottom level.

"Hey," he says, "would you like to use my room for a couple of days? It's a little bit larger."

"You're sweet to offer, but I just need to conk out in the cramped corner I call home. My guess is I'll be asleep before I hit the board."

"Will you call me when you wake up? And if you don't mind, I'd like to take your key with me. If I don't hear from you in, let's say, three hours, I'm coming down to check on you."

I smile at that. "It's a concussion where you're supposed to wake people up every few hours, not an almost-drowning. But go ahead—I'd like you to come by, and I'll feel more secure having you check on me."

I give him my key and he lets us in, then pockets it.

"Just one more thing," he says.

"That's Columbo's line."

"We could use him. But I just want to know before I leave you—is there any reason you can think of why someone would be after you? Please don't make light of this, Ruby."

"Let's just say I know we need to have a talk, Ed. I'll be wide awake in a few hours. This cabin's pretty stuffy for a long talk, but if I'm feeling yukky, maybe we'll just hole up here. Otherwise, we can find someplace private. But I don't want my story to be interrupted, not by anybody."

"You realize you're scaring me? I'm about ready to camp outside the door here."

"It'll wait. And I'm warning you—I'm not the only one who's going to talk tonight. You're going to answer some questions, too."

"What do you mean?"

"I mean you're holding back a lot from me, and don't think for a minute I don't know it."

"Did you ever think it might be for your own safety? Now, more than ever?"

"No one's going to know we're having this talk tonight. There comes a point where we're going to have to trust each other. Go home and think about it while I fall in bed, okay?"

"I'd rather think about your falling in bed, but I get the message."

I give him a long hug and a short kiss. "Later."

"Later."

I crawl under the covers after he leaves, turn my head away from the light coming in the porthole, and try to think about what happened to me. The next thing I know, I wake up to a dark room, hearing a knock on the door.

"Can I come in?"

"Ed?"

He puts the key in the lock and turns on one of the lights.

"Are you okay? I didn't want to wait any longer without checking on you."

"Did you forget something?"

"No, you forgot everything. You've been asleep for three and a half hours. It's nighttime, if you hadn't noticed."

"I slept like the dead." Bad analogy. I'm awake enough to remember now.

"It's about nine o'clock," he says. "Can I bring you something to eat? Or would you feel like getting some fresh air on deck?"

"Maybe a little of both. But you'd have to promise to find somewhere totally private."

"Our place by the lifeboats would be best. Your Temple Rita group is watching a feature film—it started just a few minutes ago, so we should be safe for a couple of hours."

"Did you think about what I said? That this will have to be a two-way confessional? Otherwise, it's no use going through the motions, Ed."

"Yeah, I'm ready to talk to you, too. This afternoon catapulted me into a different space than just our karaoke-room date the other night. I want to make sure nothing like that ever happens again."

"Well, I can't disagree with that. Give me a minute and I'll be ready. Why don't you see if you can round up some sandwiches and Cokes in the kitchen, and I'll meet you at our rail. Do you still have my key?"

"Here, take it. I'd tell you to get ready at your own pace, but we might only have a couple of hours. Although I think they're having a film trivia quiz afterward."

"I'll hurry. I'm anxious to get out of this cramped room, too—it's not good for much besides sleeping."

We meet at our place on deck and spread out our picnic of turkey sandwiches, chips, and Cokes. Nothing has ever tasted this good—I haven't eaten for hours. I feel rested and relaxed, until I remember our agenda for tonight.

"I should have asked earlier," Ed says. "Do you have a headache or anything? Are you up for this?"

"I'm feeling great and rested, as a matter of fact, but I don't know how long it will last. So let me go first—then I can just listen to your part."

"Shoot." He leans back against the rail and stretches his legs out on the deck—jeans and sneakers with no socks. I've thrown on the first thing I reached for in the cabin—khaki shorts and one of our Hot Bagel baseball team shirts.

"I realize I don't know where to start," I say.

"Start with why someone would want to push you down in the water. When I asked you that earlier, I sensed you knew exactly why."

"Not exactly—certainly not why someone would want me dead. But it might have something to do with the old synagogue we visited the other day in the rain."

Ed tenses up as soon as the words get out of my mouth, but he doesn't interrupt.

"I wanted photos of the inside of the building, so when I was in the temple backyard, I stood up on an old drum, held my digital camera over my head, and took three blind shots through a hole in one of the boarded-up windows. That used up the camera's internal memory, and before I got down, I put in an extra memory card to use for some exterior shots. Before I knew what happened, I was down on the ground with a knot on my skull that hurt like hell. I thought I might have slipped and fallen, but I realized it wasn't like that—someone had kicked the drum from under me, hit me on the head, and taken the memory card out of my camera. When I came to my senses, the card slot door was neatly closed, but the card was gone."

Ed's leaning toward me, and his eyes couldn't stretch any wider if he were trying. "You didn't tell anybody or report this? Why . . . ?"

"Just listen as you said you would. When I got back to the ship, I hooked up the camera to my little computer and saw that two of the photos were duds—just black—and the third was a good flash shot of a leather briefcase in the middle of all the renovation rubble. It was the same leather briefcase I saw your friend holding when you two met near that landmark Lutheran church the other day. I'm absolutely positive of that—it was a Coach British tan leather case like one I'd seen in a shop window in town, and I was only a few houses away from you—very close. That was the day you claimed not to have seen when I waved, or heard me call you."

"Ruby, I can't believe I'm hearing this. Don't you realize—"

"I'd love to make this a dialogue, but I'm afraid I'll wind down. I just have one other thing to say."

"Okay." He keeps his eyes fastened on me like a vise, but he's quiet while I finish.

"Why did you erase files from the professor's laptop?"

Ed looks as if I've just run over him with a steamroller. He waits before he answers, head down with his hands over his ears. Talk about body language—I think he's trying to deny what he just heard. Finally he looks up.

"I'm speechless," he says. "Anything I say is going to be

too much. It's so much more complex than I want to go into . . ."

"Or than my pretty little head can comprehend? Try me."

As usual, I'm not helping my cause, so I'd better apologize. "Sorry. I didn't give you a chance to finish, did I?"

"That's the least of it. I just can't believe that in a few days as a tourist you've managed to get into all this. And that you said nothing."

"So now instead of answering my questions, you're attacking me for finding out, right? For stumbling into something . . ."

"Something you know nothing about."

"Not for long. You can bet on that."

I lean forward to make my point, and I feel a pair of well-tanned arms ending in long red fingernails wrapping around my shoulders, followed by short, hairy arms grabbing my waist.

"I've got her first! I touched Ruby first, so I get to bring her in. Your touch doesn't count, Rabbi."

Essie Sue is dragging me backward in a choke hold, while Kevin clings to my waist. The result is like being placed on a medieval rack with the crank turning.

"No, I got to her first. The scavenger list said 'Redhead,' and I immediately thought of Ruby. I saw you following me, Essie Sue."

"Wrong. Tell him, Ruby—you felt me on you first, didn't you? I grabbed your shoulders way before he got here."

"No one gets me until you let go—I'm warning you."

They both drop me at the same time, leaving me lying on the deck in a prone position.

"What is this? Are you two nuts?"

"The movie they showed was a documentary on growing corn—it was a cost-cutting measure, and it came free from the Department of Agriculture," Kevin says. "Essie Sue made us stay and watch it."

"I did until it got too boring," she says. "Then I remembered they were having a scavenger hunt on A Deck, so we signed up. The last thing we have to find is one redhead, and you're mine, Ruby. You have to come with me to the social committee so they can check you off the list."

"I'm getting credit for her, too." Kevin's dragging me his way.

"Nothing doing, folks—I'm busy."

"Okay," Kevin says, "but you're not going to like it when we have to bring the whole committee here to prove we found you. And besides, they have to decide if both of us can get credit."

Ed pulls me aside. "Go, already," he says. "I'm too bummed out to talk right now, Ruby. You're going to have to let me absorb everything you've hit me with before I can answer."

"You're just using this as a convenient excuse."

"Right now, it's a godsend. I promise you some answers if you'll promise me not to be alone tonight—I want you to stay around other people, and I'll catch up with you before the evening's over."

"What choice do I have? I can tell you, though, that I'm already exhausted from all this, despite the sleep I had this afternoon. I'm turning in early."

"Just lock your door from the inside."

"Ruby, if you don't come with us right now, we'll lose our points. Kevin can go find the committee if you want."

"No, I give up. I'm coming."

It figures—just when I'm feeling totally worthless, I'm somebody's prize.

As if I weren't already a marked woman, the social director stamps an X on my forehead in washable ink as soon as I arrive on A Deck. Essie Sue has to share the point with Kevin, making them eligible for a tiebreaker.

"You have to stay until the winner is declared," Essie Sue says. "They say the prize is really huge."

I'll bet—on a ship that gets movies from the Department of Agriculture. But Ed looked so awful when I left him that I don't much relish the idea of going to my cabin and obsessing about all this. I really do want him to absorb what I've said tonight—it's the only way I'm going to get anything out of him.

As the two finalists, Essie Sue and Kevin have one more item to bring back. Mr. Chernoff gets the honor of drawing the selection—it's a Palm Pilot, any model. I have to stay with the committee while the finalists see who can find one first.

"I'm knocking on all doors," Essie Sue says, and she's off.

Kevin says nothing, but takes off down the corridor

after her. Lots of luck if he thinks he can talk her into sharing this one. The only reason the contest is tied at all is because I told her I'd swear that they both touched me at the same time.

We only have to wait about five minutes when Kevin comes running back with one of the little handheld organizers. He holds it up and lets the social director check it off.

"The rules are that I don't have to tell where I got this, right?" he asks her.

"That's the rule," she says. "You're responsible for putting it back after the contest."

"Then I'm the winner!" he says. "Wait'll Essie Sue finds out."

"Congratulations, Kevin," I say. Anytime Essie Sue's a loser is a good day in my book.

"What did I win?"

"We have to wait until the other contestant comes back."

Which isn't long. Essie Sue runs in beaming and tosses a Palm Pilot on the table. "I had to pay someone to lend me this, but I did it."

"You're too late," Kevin says. "I won."

Uh-oh. This woman's ears are not wired for that response. She doesn't hear it.

"I said, I won. I brought back a Palm Pilot in five minutes."

"Impossible." She heard it but she's not buying it.

"The rules say I don't have to tell how."

"No matter," the social director says. "Rabbi Kapstein is the winner, and he can now step forward for his prize."

Kevin stands up to applause—his favorite thing to do—and receives a wrapped package that's about two feet wide and three feet high. He rips it open to reveal a huge—yep, they said it would be huge—autographed photo of Captain Goldberg at the wheel of the ship.

"Wow," I say. "Now that's a treasure." Wonder what the loser gets.

"I can't believe you won over me," Essie Sue says. "And what a wonderful memento of the voyage—I'd be thrilled to have it."

"You can have it," Kevin says. "What can I do with it?" He's underwhelmed with the gift, as well he might be.

"I'd love it," she says, "unless Ruby might want it—I'd be willing to give it up under certain circumstances."

"Uh—I can't think what those circumstances would be, Essie Sue." Or let's just say I can't bear to. "You're welcome to it."

Essie Sue's not giving up on the contest. "Rabbi, I still don't understand where you got a Palm Pilot so fast—they're not that easy to come by."

"I'm not going to tell her," he whispers to me. "Let her keep guessing."

"It's driving her crazy," I say, "and I'm curious, too. Where *did* you get it?"

"Maybe I'll tell you before we go home, and maybe not."

Fine. Game-playing with Kevin is not something I

want to waste my time on. I get the social director to wipe the red mark off my forehead and I'm off. No use expecting to be thanked by either Kevin or Essie Sue for my trouble. These are the same people who knew I almost drowned today and haven't yet asked me how I'm feeling.

As for how I *am* feeling, the answer is, lousy. It's close to eleven o'clock and I realize the three hours' rest I had before Ed woke me wasn't enough. I want more sleep, and I want it now. When I go to my room, I see that he's slipped a note under the door:

> *Let's make it tomorrow. Don't give up on me——it* will *happen.*
> *Ed*
>
> *P.S.* Please *lock your door from the inside tonight.*

It's just as well——as much as I want to hear his response, I can't deal with it tonight. And what *will* happen? Is he going to tell the whole story?

30

I look for Ed at breakfast, but he's nowhere to be seen. I'll find him later and pin him down one way or the other, but meanwhile I'm taking his advice and sticking with other people today instead of taking off by myself. I sit down at Sara's table just as she's ordering.

"I've learned that they can't ruin cornflakes," she says.

I heartily agree, and skip the elaborate culinary descriptions of Neptune's Eggs (two soft-boiled eggs that are supposed to be hard, or vice versa, nestled in faux egg cups made of that black seaweed they put around sushi rolls); Buccaneer's Bacon (two limp pieces of turkey bacon that some unfortunate cook's assistant has actually braided with his or her own hands—an event I'd rather not visualize); and English Muffin à la Mermaid (a sardine sandwich with the tails sticking out).

I start to order plain oatmeal but think better of it— I'm safer with something that has spent no time at all out of the box.

"I'll take a serving-sized carton of Shredded Wheat, please, and a half-pint container of skim milk."

The waiter takes my order and notes that there's been a big run on boxed cereal lately. I just hope they have lots of it in the pantry.

"Where's Jack?"

"He went fishing today, and I'm on my own. Want to explore something together?"

"Sure."

It's odd to me that with all the fanfare yesterday, she hasn't mentioned my incident in the water. I'm certainly not looking for attention, but if it were the other way around, I know I'd be asking a zillion questions as well as expressing concern. Of course, that's *my* curse. Maybe Sara was blessed with the discretion I seem to have missed out on.

"You know, I'd love to see the old synagogue. We had other plans the day your temple group visited there."

"It poured that day, Sara, and the trip wasn't very productive. They're renovating the place, and most of it is locked up tight. We did get to see some of the exterior, though, and I liked climbing up to where the building nestles into the hillside. That's about it—maybe we could find something else to visit—someplace that's open."

After all that's happened, a trip to the synagogue on Crystal Gade is definitely off my agenda for today. For all I know, people might be watching the place. I shudder when I think of that stormy morning.

It feels peculiar for me to know so much I can't share with anyone but Nan, or with Ed if we ever discover a level playing field. All these secrets are even coloring my attitude toward spending the morning with Sara. I can't really relax with her today, and the idea of being together seems more like a big chore. This is no way to live.

"Why don't we walk around downtown, Ruby? We can visit one of the open markets—I'm sure they're not elegant enough for You-Know-Who and Company, so we won't be bothered."

"Great idea. I don't have a lot of energy this morning, anyway, and that fits my mood."

Still, no comment about yesterday's adventure, if you can call it that.

It's hot already, but the flea market is crowded—the weather hasn't stopped anyone. We spend an hour poking our noses into everything from island herbal remedies to schlock Rolex watches, comfortable with each other's pace. Someone has set up an air-conditioned tent with tables, and we stop by to find a cool drink.

"You were going to tell me more about your genealogy project," I say.

"Just a feeling I had that some of my ancestors were

Jewish, but I think there's a much better chance that Jack's are."

"Really? You're active Catholics, aren't you? Why would you even think of exploring in that direction?"

"I guess you could call it an accident. As I mentioned, it was my own family I had a hunch about—a totally irrational hunch, really, except that I've always had this affinity for Jewish people. A couple of my best friends in high school were Jewish, and I felt this special kinship with them."

"And your search didn't yield much?"

"No, not really, nor did my questions to older family members. But when I got on the Net, I came in contact with people whose great-grandparents had lived in the same area as Jack's family. I made some inquiries and discovered that there were certain family names, his among them, that were common to the Conversos who were scattered throughout that area. When I remembered stories his grandmother had told me as a bride about the family's life in Mexico, some of them rang a bell. They were odd tales—terribly similar to some of the rural experiences the rabbi's been lecturing about."

"I gather you said something to Jack and he was less than enthused?"

"I didn't say anything to Jack for ages—I did repeat some of the tales, but I didn't reference them to his family in any way. I figured he'd recognize the similarities himself, and tell me about them. He didn't, even though I knew this was family history he was familiar with."

"Why didn't you just ask straight-out?"

"First, because his grandmother was peculiar and secretive about this stuff—she said she just wanted me to know, but that no one in the family was really interested in the ceremonies performed so many years ago. Since Jack had never mentioned any of this, I let it go. He's such a devoutly religious man, I thought it might disturb him."

"What if it had?"

"You know what a long-term marriage is like, Ruby. You just sense certain areas to stay away from."

Well, maybe she did, but I sure didn't—sometimes to Stu's annoyance, but so what? There was nothing we couldn't talk about at one point or another. Agreeing on it was another matter, but that's part of the give and take.

"So what does he think you're doing now when you research this topic on-line, or doesn't he know?"

"At first, just that I was interested in my ancestors. But I have something else to tell you, Ruby."

"If you think I can help you in some way, go ahead. But if it's going to make trouble for you, maybe you ought to reconsider."

"I need to talk about it."

"I'm a pretty good listener."

"It wasn't an accident that we came on this cruise. I met Professor Gonzales on-line, or I should say, I heard about him on-line. I e-mailed him and asked if he ever got to El Paso on his lecture tours. He said no, but that he did lecture for cruises, and that the Bitmans had booked him as lecturer for the temple group, with Captain Goldberg's permission. He mentioned that the cruise was open to individuals, aside from various tour groups onboard. I gave him our names, and was looking forward to his lectures. Jack and I take a vacation every year around this time, anyway, and I usually make the arrangements. It wasn't hard to suggest the Caribbean."

"You must have been as shocked as we were, then, when the professor had a heart attack."

"I felt awful. In fact, I was so shocked, I let something slip about how gracious he was to me on-line. Immediately, I realized what I'd said, and I expected Jack to lose his temper. He didn't. The thing he was most concerned about was that I not talk about having been in contact with him. He said it was about my private family business, and that I shouldn't get involved. He was pretty persuasive— it sounded reasonable to me, so I didn't."

"Seems as though you don't have any decisions to make, then."

Sara waits until the waiter pours us more tea.

"But I do. Part of me wants to tell Jack that it's his family I've found out about, not mine."

"Do you really think you'll be surprising him? You've already told him that some of those practices might have been a holdover from Jews driven out of Spain during the Inquisition. Even if he thought you were researching your own roots, he obviously knows his own family stories. He's not dumb. He's probably put two and two together already, and decided he wants it to equal zero. We're not a beloved minority, Sara, despite the good vibes you experienced with Jews. Maybe it's a threat to Jack to even consider that his Catholicism isn't ninety-nine forty-four percent pure."

"I don't want to piss him off, though."

Now I'm ready to end this conversation—this subject isn't part of my repertoire.

"Then don't."

"Would you?"

"Sara, maybe it's temperament, or maybe it's a WASP thing—except that you're Catholic. I don't know enough about you to say. I tell what I think even to strangers, so if Jack were my husband, why would I hold back from my most intimate confidant? Unless he isn't, and that's your business, too, not mine."

"I know you're right. And he is proud of his Christian heritage in an exclusive way that I don't share. He belonged to a men's business club that took in women only three years ago and then realized to its surprise that they had no Jews, either. I know he's not bigoted personally, but he's very conscious of his station in life, and of the fact that he worked his way up to his position today."

"In other words, he might consider your discoveries about his family to be life-changing, but not in the way you'd hope."

Well, this answers my question about why the Marquezes' names appeared on the professor's list. I must say the whole disclosure hasn't brought me closer to these people. Sara's wimpiness is irritating even though there's lots about her I like, and I've heard more about Jack's attitudes than I want to know. All I want to do now is go back to bed.

31

"I hear Essie Sue's looking for you," Ed says.

"Oh, I'm sure she is. She wants our whole group to go to the costume party as one—one *what,* she won't tell us. I haven't been interested, frankly."

We've found an alcove on the very top deck tonight, where it's quiet and fairly private. We're removed from the crowd noises, except for the faint sound of some big-band music coming from below. The moon is quite blazingly visible from our perch, and lights up a path on the water. The scene would be incredibly romantic if we weren't preparing for a bunch of unpleasant revelations.

"I just want you to know that I'm accepting no inter-ruptions," I say—"no inexplicable disappearances, no sud-den forays after something you've forgotten below. If you drop dead here on the spot, I'm getting some answers from your dead body, Levinger."

"Ferocious," he says, "but I swear, I'm yours."

"I know you're an investigative reporter in San Antonio, not a travel writer. So what are you investi-gating?"

"That's not quite fair. I have done investigative pieces, but I've written travel articles as well, some of them, as I told you, about the Caribbean. Why shouldn't I take advantage of a chance for a vacation if I can wangle the assignment?"

"So you're starting off as a hostile witness, huh? Okay, at least I know where I stand. Maybe I can market a piece of my own, complete with pictures."

"I need to know about that photo you took, Ruby, for your own safety. You don't see me being the object of attackers, do you? The focus here is on you, not me."

"You talk about my safety. How can I get any help from you if I don't even know who you are? I mean it, Ed—either you level with me, or I'm relying on my own sources."

"What sources?" We're both sitting on the deck facing each other with our legs folded in front of us.

"Damn it. Quit interviewing me. I've spoken to other people—you ought to know that for openers."

"Okay, Ruby. I am investigating something for the

paper, but I can't tell you what it is. Yet. Now, can you tell me who you've spoken to?"

"Someone in my local police department." This doesn't make the blinding impression I thought it would.

"Well, the long arm of your police department hasn't prevented an attempt on your life, has it? I'm here—they're there. Tell me about the picture."

"I guess it isn't necessary to add that your being here didn't prevent anything, either, Ed. Who were you meeting with the other day, and why was his briefcase left in the old synagogue?"

"I'm not sure why, Ruby—I was as surprised as you were that it was there. In fact, you may have helped in my own inquiry by letting me know the briefcase *was* there. You were taking the photo because . . . ?"

"I was just trying to get an interior shot so the day wouldn't be a total loss."

"Then so far, we know that someone was watching you and removed the electronic memory card from your camera so the location of that briefcase wouldn't be revealed. And when there was no image on the memory card, they wanted to make sure you couldn't be an eyewitness, either. I'm sure they think you're more involved than you actually were when you took that photo."

"The photo's safe, by the way. It's back in Texas and erased from everything here—camera, computer, and card. If anything happens to me, it *will* surface."

"Good."

He looks as if he means it—I was half expecting him

to grill me about the photo's whereabouts. Either he wants to appear cool about the possibility that the police have it, which they don't yet, or he's really thinking I did the right thing for my protection. Which reminds me . . .

"Speaking of erasing, Ed, tell me again why you erased the professor's files from his laptop. And please don't insult my intelligence by telling me you don't know what I'm talking about, okay? We were interrupted last time I asked."

"Tell *me* again how you know about that."

"Because I copied them to my own computer. They're in Texas, too." They're not, but I feel safer saying they are. "And I happened to look at the laptop a few days ago and noticed that a third of them had been erased. You and I were the only ones who handled that machine besides Kevin."

"That you know of."

Well, he's right there, but I know he did it.

"Yeah, I erased them," he says.

I breathe an inaudible sigh of relief—at least we're now down to the real thing, not bull.

"Mainly," he says, "I didn't want anyone getting ahold of the information. If the guy's dead, he certainly won't need it, the rabbi's clueless, and it could be downright dangerous for some outsider to have it. Like you, for instance. It hasn't improved your risk factors, has it? You got knocked on the head, robbed, and almost drowned. Is that explanation enough?"

"Nothing had happened to me when you deleted those files. Why did you think they were dangerous? Certainly nothing on their face indicated that—I've gone over and over them."

"Ruby, I can't tell you that. We can negotiate some things, but not others. My investigation told me that there could be some danger, that's all. Even I haven't figured out why the particular information on that computer means so much to someone. Ask me something else."

"Like you're really telling me anything. But okay, I'll keep asking. What part of the files are you puzzled over? For myself, I couldn't understand the references to passwords. I didn't understand the Marquez references, either, but I think I've solved that one."

"How?"

"Sara Marquez told me she'd contacted the professor about some of their family history—she thinks one of them might have been descended from the Conversos Willie Bob was researching. Membership in the tribe might threaten a lifestyle Jack Marquez values, I'm guessing. Do you think Gonzales could have been blackmailing him?"

"It's a thought. I'll look into it, Ruby."

"That's it?"

"It's possible that could turn out to be true, but if I give you any definitive answers, I'd have to reveal more about what I've discovered than I want you to know right now."

"That really helps a lot."

"Sorry. Maybe we can put our heads together on the password issue, Ruby. I looked in the Windows password file on the laptop, but I couldn't find anything remotely useful. There is no password protection enabled on that computer."

"But did you see the note he made to himself that said, 'If something happens, see who controls the Flight Simulator program'? I looked, and there is no such program installed."

"Yeah, I saw the note. That's a game that's also used as a flight training program for small planes. Even for small jets," he says. "And I think it would be a stretch to assume that the phrase 'If something happens' refers to something happening to *him,* don't you?"

"Except for the fact that something *did* happen to him—he had a heart attack and died."

"The whole note is too tenuous, Ruby. We're going to have to find more before it can mean anything."

"Okay, then, let's get back to the briefcase in the temple. Do you think it had money in it?"

He's quiet—thinking about whether or not to let me in on this, I guess. I keep my mouth shut for a change, giving him some time to decide.

"It's possible the temple was used as a drop point," he says. "If you're already thinking money and briefcase, then some sort of payoff is an obvious conclusion, isn't it? So I'm not telling you much if I agree that it does sound like a drop-off was in progress. I didn't know about the temple until you told me, but I did suspect there was going to be a payoff in this operation at some point. I just wish it had been me who'd looked inside that building."

"Is this a drug deal?"

"I'm not saying. But don't jump to the conclusion that it is, just because I can't answer."

"Who was the man you were meeting near Government House?"

"Just someone who I thought might help me in researching this. I figured he knew something, and, obviously, he did."

"When can I know as much as you do?"

"Eventually, it's all going to come out. But for now, there's not a chance in hell I'm going to blow this by leaking it to you. It's just not gonna happen."

"How do I know you're not connected to it? Other than as a reporter?"

"I assume you've been holding back all along because you aren't sure of me. That was probably prudent. But now we're in a peculiar situation where we both need to trust each other to a certain extent. Yet neither of us can be sure of how far to go. I think we should concentrate on solving the issues that occur to us both. If there's anything you haven't told me that you think might help me, please don't hold back."

"Well, for one thing, I have the police back home checking to see if Willie Bob's death was truly a heart attack. He seems to be at the center of this."

"I've been wondering about that, too, in light of some

of the files I read. He not only has information on lots of people in there, but there are these odd references to other material that's possibly hidden. Maybe we should go through the files together."

"We've both combed through them. I don't know what another go-through would produce."

"Then let's at least examine them by ourselves one more time, and make a list of questions that pop up."

It's hard for me to believe Ed's not on the right side of this business, but maybe I'm the wrong person to be speculating. As if he were reading my mind, he suddenly sits back and looks at me.

"Ruby, you do understand that my chief concern now is that you're kept safe. So far, no one knows that we've found suspicious computer files, even though someone does realize that you photographed the drop-off site. I have some backup sources, too, and I've let them know what's happened to you. We just haven't figured out what to do about it yet."

He pulls me over by him and we look out at the water from our high perch. I feel safe with his arm around me, but remote from him, too, and I know he feels that.

"I want to kiss you like the other night," he says, "but that was an innocent time compared to now. I'm sensing that it wouldn't be welcome. I don't like rejection, and especially from you, so I'm wary. Am I right?"

"It's not that it wouldn't be welcome. It's just that we wouldn't be in sync like we ought to be. That's important enough for me to wait. But just for your information, I'm not happy about it."

He keeps his arm around me, and squeezes my shoulder. For now, it's enough.

32

"Quit talking, ladies and gentlemen. We have business to discuss."

Our group leaders have called a meeting of the Temple Rita contingent in the middle of the afternoon—all of us are assembled in the dining room to make plans for the captain's Costume Ball and Final Banquet. The Final Banquet is also show-off time for the crew, in preparation for those big tips we're expected to dispense. That's when the wine steward, whose only contact with most of us has been his speech on the first night touting the *Bargain II* Zinfandel Special—priced at $22.95 and worth a third of that—stops at every table to pose for pictures and profess friendship for life.

Essie Sue has finished her lecture on tipping (don't spoil the help) and is about to begin her speech on group unity. Letty Levy inquires as to why the concept of unity requires that we all wriggle under a heavy tarp to represent a moving centipede.

"That was a nasty rumor, Letty, and certainly not in the spirit of our pilgrimage here."

This is the first time I've heard this tour referred to as a pilgrimage, but I decide to let sleeping clichés lie in the interest of unity.

"What I conceive, people, is something much more dramatic—a live Star of David, with all of us dressed alternately in blue and white."

"You mean like marbles on an Israeli Parcheesi board?" At the risk of adding yet another cliché, let's just say that Bubba Copeland doesn't suffer fools gladly.

"I'll ignore any spoilsports—this idea is way too fabulous to be destroyed by the likes of a Copeland brother. All in favor?"

I raise my hand—a lone phoenix in a sea of ashes.

"Ruby Rothman! I'm amazed, dear—you're always so negative. See, people? Ruby thinks this is a good idea. Please share your thoughts with those who, shall we say, are not so swift?"

"I just figured it was a good way to get out of dreaming up a costume on my own."

All hands go up. It appears they aren't so dumb after all.

I feel a tap on my shoulder. A slimy tap.

Captain Goldberg's already sparse blond locks must

have gone from plural to singular on this voyage, because he's now sporting a curly platinum hairpiece that's slightly askew. The wig is so odd that I'm truly curious about it, but not curious enough to risk an actual interchange with him. I'm trying to ignore his fingers drumming their way up my neck, hoping that if I just move away silently at first and get some distance between us, I can make a run for it soon.

He raises one hand to be recognized by his cousin Essie Sue, at the same time grabbing my hair with the other one, which had just been grazing my neck.

"Did you wish to speak, Horatio?" Essie Sue's beaming.

"I just want to compliment this lovely lady here for her leadership abilities—she's apparently won over the whole assembly. I'd like to announce to all of you that Miss Ruby is my first choice for Cruise Queen at the Costume Ball on our final night. Since she'll obviously want to be out-fitted for this glorious occasion, I don't think you should count on her as a mere cog in your assembled wheel. The animated Star of David will have to do without her lively presence."

"That's thrilling, Captain. As your only relative on-board, I'll be glad to help prepare her for the occasion." Essie Sue attempts to lead the applause, but there is none. They're all looking at *moi*.

Aside from the fact that Miss Ruby the Cruise Queen sounds like something out of Times Square before Mayor Giuliani got there, this only proves to me that we ought to put Essie Sue and Horatio's family genes under a microscope—in case of nuclear war, they'll be the only things left besides the cockroaches. After the kick I gave that man, he's still coming back for more?

I look up at, presumably, the Cruise King, smile sweetly, and say only to him, "Get your fingers out of my hair or your blond rug is history, Horatio." He does, and fast.

To the silent audience, I merely say, "I decline the honor."

"Oh, she always says that, Cousin— don't pay her any attention. She'll be at the ball with bells on."

Cowbells, if Essie Sue has anything to do with it, I'm sure.

Horatio snaps his fingers and one of his burly minions comes rushing over to escort him out of the room. He's so taken with himself I've never even seen him standing alone without his crew prancing around him. I call him the Royal Wee. Before he leaves, though, he turns around and winks at me. The only person who could truly appreciate this is Nan. I'd run over to the Internet café tonight and e-mail her if I weren't being supercautious. Tomorrow.

33

E-mail from: Ruby
To: Nan
Subject: *Lunacy Update*

I'm writing this in the early morning again—anything to escape the *Bargain II* breakfast. I'm getting a lot of network interference, so this'll be quick.

Aside from wanting you to know that I've been nominated as Cruise Queen by none other than Captain Horatio, the Date to Hate, I also need to fill you in on the mutual Truth session I had last night with Ed.

Not much came of it, but he admitted
that he erased the computer files because
he didn't want anyone (like me) getting
hold of them. After I told him I knew
he was an investigative reporter, he did
say that he wasn't writing a travel
article. That's all I could get out of
him about what he *is* doing—he says it's
for my own safety.

It just occurs to me that I ought to
send this before my connection is wiped
out and so that I can see if you've written to me.

More in a minute.

E-mail from: Nan
To: Ruby
Subject: *Paul*

Wanted you to know asap that Paul's
investigation produced some unexpected
results—Willie Bob Gonzales didn't die
of a heart attack. The lab found potassium chloride in the body, and needle
marks where the substance had been
injected. Potassium chloride mimics the
symptoms of a heart attack, and there's
no question that someone deliberately
used it to try and get away with murder. Your ship will be held at the port
in Galveston when you arrive, and no
passengers will be allowed to disembark
without interrogation. The Galveston

police believe it's prudent to keep these procedures secret until the *Bargain II* sails into the harbor.

Paul was glad to be able to get in touch with you through me, since any other means of communication directly to the ship could be compromised. And, of course, since the death took place on Texas soil before the ship sailed for the Caribbean, there's no doubt about jurisdiction—in other words, no worry about the laws of the sea, whatever they might be.

Paul says to please be careful and stay with the group. And you know already that I'll be sick with worry until you call me safe and sound from port.

Love, Me

E-mail from: Ruby
To: Nan
Subject: *Go It Alone?*

So now that it's official, what do I do? This is a rhetorical question, because I don't think I'll be getting down here anymore in the mornings to hear from you. Tomorrow night's the costume party, and the next day we sail for Galveston. But since I'm here now, I might as well try to absorb this news by writing back to you and thinking aloud.

Ed suspected along with me that maybe the professor was murdered. He knows more about the briefcase than I do, but we both think it's been used in a money drop at the old synagogue. He says my unlucky observation of the temple interior helped him in his own investigation—he hadn't known that was the dropping-off place.

I do believe him, Nan, that he's holding back for my protection. The curious part of me wants to be informed of everything that's going on, but the other part feels safer not knowing for now. I don't know whether to hole up and wait this out, or to tell Ed what Paul passed on to me. Wish you were here so I could pick your brain.

I hope the next communication from me will be from Texas soil!

34

The air is cool in my cabin for a change as I slip into my costume for the living Star of David. Despite what the captain said, I'm a blue cog in the giant wheel—blue-jean shorts, blue polo shirt, and even the blue and white sneakers I happened to have with me. In other words, *très* comfortable—I lucked out. I'm looking forward to tonight's fairwell Costume Ball because it means the cruise from hell will be over by tomorrow night.

We disembark at the Port of Galveston sometime before twelve—probably nine or ten, the porter tells me. If the recent history of this barge is any indication, I'll be happy to touch land by midnight. I have no idea what will happen after that, though. If the police want us confined, we could possibly spend another night on the ship, which would be horrible. With the best scenario, we'll be questioned and let go, with instructions to remain in touch if we're needed.

Even though we flew to Galveston for our departure, Essie Sue chartered a bus for our return trip when she realized we might not make the last flight to Austin via Houston. Now we'll probably end up driving all night to Eternal, but that'll be fine with me—just beam me home.

I'm on my way into the dining room, ready for the Final Banquet, when someone pulls me into one of the adjacent lounges. Essie Sue.

"Good, Ruby—I'm glad you aren't dressed yet. I've got a surprise for you."

"But I am dressed—I'm one of the blue people. Looks like you're white." She's wearing one of her snow-white pantsuits, silk, expensive, and pristine.

"The rabbi and I will be with the white contingent," she says. "But, you—much more is in store for you."

She puts one hand over my eyes while the other unveils something from a plastic bag hanging over the doorway. It's a costume Elizabeth I might have worn if she'd hocked the empire—rhinestones and sequins over rayon with heavy metallic edging. This thing must weigh fifty pounds, and it's an alarming purple color.

"This is your outfit. The captain paid for it."

"I declined, remember?"

"I picked it out before we left for the trip—that's how

long I've had to keep the secret, Ruby. Horatio knew from the start that you were going to be his Cruise Queen."

"He didn't even know me."

"But he'd heard. I told him all about you before the voyage, and persuaded him to spend some of the ship's funds on the costume."

"From what I've seen on this ship, Essie Sue, he wouldn't part with a dime."

"*Au contraire,* he's been very generous. He said to spend whatever I wanted to on it, and he'd reimburse me."

"And has he?"

"Has he paid me back? I'm getting the money tonight."

"Don't hold your breath, Essie Sue."

"You're too pessimistic—remember, he's part of my family."

"I know only too well. See ya."

I run right into the arms of Kevin, who's really gifted in blocking doorways.

"Hold her, Rabbi—she's not ready."

"Me, not ready? Kevin's still in the sheets."

"That's my toga. I didn't have anything white, so Essie Sue fixed me up like a Roman in bedsheets."

Why do I ask? That draping job could only have been done by Essie Sue—he must be wearing a thousand pins.

I duck under his arm-drape and head for the dining room, to witness a scene that must have been the model for the phrase *motley crew*. The dining staff are dressed as ragtag varieties of sea life—I've never seen seen so many gaping fish. These costumes must have been worn for hundreds of cruises, though—they even smell like fish.

The passengers, with the exception of our blue-and-white bunch, have followed the brochure's instructions and brought along the usual store-bought varieties of pirates, ghosts, witches, and Nixon heads—these *après* Halloween specials far outnumber anything else. The dining room is one big Disney *Fantasia,* with the emphasis on cartoons.

Unfortunately, the food can't be disguised. We're getting everything they couldn't push down our throats on all the other nights. The culinary theme is Embarrassment of Riches Assortment. It's an embarrassment, all right, but I'd call it Pathetic Leftovers. Things dyed blue weren't too popular on those early Fiesta Fantasy Nights, so those have been hauled out of the freezer, complemented by the breakfast tacos no one chose to eat. There were no desserts left, so we're stuck with heaping bowls of prunes.

Captain Goldberg is presiding over it all, dressed like George III in his mad period. A white wig with curls falling to his shoulders caps the velvet outfit he's wearing. If you ask me, the royal robes have seen one too many coronations—he should have stuck with his uniform. Who knows what animal species that velour is housing? I hope they're serving Raid at his table.

Speaking of the captain's table, I suddenly realize I'm probably expected to sit there as queen, so I skip the delicious eats. I grab an unopened can of cola and a sealed

packet of soda crackers—you can never be too careful—
and head for the open breeze. So far, no one in authority
has figured out how to spoil the sea air.

Essie Sue's right behind me.

"Ruby, this has gone too far. You *have* to be the Cruise
Queen—Horatio's counting on you. With all the cost-
cutting measures, what if his salary is reduced, or he loses
his job? We can't have rumors that he's lost his leadership
touch."

"Lost his touch? The man's lost, all right, and I definitely don't want his touch. You can be the queen."

"I can't wear this costume—it's two sizes too big."

"You mean you wouldn't be caught dead in it, cousin
or no cousin."

"Do you want to be responsible for his losing his job?
He's announced to everyone that you'll reign with him
tonight."

"That's not fair. I don't want the man to get fired, but
I'm not dancing with him at any ball."

"Okay. You won't have to dance. Just stay up there for
the coronation, and you're finished."

"How long will it take?"

"Five minutes."

"What's in it for me?"

"How about one of the free pastrami certificates?"

"The big ones that are coming into the country
through Mexico? No thanks. You'll have to do much better than that."

"How about no fund-raising activities for a whole year?"

"Now you're talking. I can't imagine what it would be like to walk into the temple for some peace and meditation while someone else worked for a change to support it. I think I deserve a sabbatical."

"You've got it. I promise not to involve you for twelve months—or maybe ten."

"A year."

"Put your arms over your head."

Geez, she's got the dress right behind her.

"You can keep your clothes on under it. I think it might be a little large."

"A little large? This thing could hold the whole English court."

When I'm so decked out I can't move, she leads me into the big dance hall. She must have timed the whole episode, because my king is waiting at the doorway for me with a microphone in his hand.

"Ruby, my dear, you look regal. Let the bugles herald our entrance," he calls out.

Two rather puny-looking horn players in the orchestra pit produce a fanfare worthy only of the *Bargain II*. No one's listening, I notice, but we proceed to the dais anyway. The captain starts to take my arm, but apparently thinks better of it. I guess he remembers that kick.

At any rate, he's only interested in the ceremonies. I can't believe anyone, not even Horatio, could get off on this nonsense, but he's beaming. One of his courtiers hands him a long scepter, and he prods me with it.

"Kneel," he says under his breath.

"No," I say under mine.

"Kneel."

Short of tripping me on the spot, he's stymied, so he finally touches the top of my head with it, knocking my crown off.

"See what you've made me do? Pick it up."

"You pick it up."

He signals one of his minions to swoop it from the ground and back onto my head.

As I look out upon my subjects, I see Temple Rita's blue-and-white drones—mostly wearing sneakers and shorts, beginning to swarm around their queen bee. Nobody's paying any attention to them, either, but, boy, do they look comfortable. I'm jealous.

"Formation One."

Essie Sue has obviously rehearsed the group with military precision. At her first bark, they all look down at the floor.

"Where are the Magic Marker spots? I don't see mine," Kevin yells. He's stepping on his neighbor Mrs. Chernoff's foot at the same time, so she's not too helpful.

"If you didn't have on that damned toga," she yells back, "you could see the floor."

Kevin stumbles over to Essie Sue, destroying Formation One, and in the process, leaves a big black mark from his kick on her white silk pants.

"Get back in line, Rabbi. You're ruining everything."

I guess she decides One is kaput, so she calls for Formation Two. At that, the group takes two steps to the left, wiping out any spectators on the sidelines but forming a tattered pattern.

If one were viewing the scene from the air, one might vaguely make out a Star of David. Then again, one might not.

No matter, because Formation Three, involving a backward step in unison, completely explodes the star and sends its pieces flying into the universe—in this case, the Black Hole being the *Bargain II* orchestra pit.

The king and I are untouched over here in our section of the galaxy. If looks could kill, though, I'd be sleeping with the fishes. His Majesty's still smarting over my failure to prostrate myself before him and be crowned.

"You certainly aren't living up to your reputation," he says. "Essie Sue told me you'd be the perfect partner on this voyage."

"Yeah, well, let's just say that as a matchmaker she's got a black thumb. If she'd tried to fix up Adam and Eve, the world would have been left with a snake and an apple. Better luck next time."

"You're not finished yet, Ruby."

"Give me a break—nobody's watching anyway."

Horatio ignores that, grabs the microphone with one hand, and waves to the band with another.

"And now, my queen, let's dance."

"Not part of the bargain," I say, as I swoosh the whole queenly outfit over my head without even having to unfasten it—that's how big it is. The crown gets caught up in the dress and comes off with everything else. I'm left as I came, pared down to my shirt, shorts, and sneakers. I'm feeling so free that I walk over to the orchestra and help the group work its way out of the pit.

Essie Sue's so busy trying to clean the sole marks from her slacks that she isn't paying the slightest attention to my abdication. I consider myself fortunate.

Not a bad exchange for a whole year off.

35

It's a perfect time to catch a breeze—they're giving out door prizes at the party and I can leave the chaos behind me. I'm on my way out to the deck when I hear footsteps a few inches away. It's Ed.

"You weren't planning to sneak up on me, were you?"

"Are you kidding?" he says. "I'm a lot of things, but not sadistic. With all you've been through, I guess you're paranoid about someone following you."

"I am. What's up?"

"Just looking for you. I got a quick glimpse of the Temple Rockettes in there, but I couldn't face the festivities. And out of the corner of my eye I did see your queen act."

"I hope you also saw me get out of it."

"Let's say I knew you'd be making an exit soon."

He looks at me with that steady gaze of his, head slightly tilted. I want to flick that loose lock of hair out of his face, but I wait, and before long, he does it himself. He takes my hand and we head for our spot on the upper floor and sit on the deck.

It's easy to forget all the bad parts of this cruise when we're looking out at the moonlight on the water.

"You know you've told me very little about yourself," I say. "I've let you know a lot more."

"You're right. If this assignment hadn't been right on top of me, I wouldn't have been so buttoned up."

"Surely you can talk about your life in San Antonio."

"You know some of it—I'm single, Jewish, driven professionally, healthy, and fairly happy. I grew up in California, but like Texas a lot better."

"Ever been married?"

"Once, a long time ago. It ended in divorce, and we had no children. My ex-wife's remarried, still lives in California, and I haven't seen her in years."

"Why didn't you remarry?"

"Never found anybody. But I do have a female Akita who's crazy about me, and it's mutual."

"An Akita—nice. You need a yard for her, yes?"

"I have a small house north of downtown, with a fenced backyard. Akitas need a good fence—they're not touchy-feely dogs, and they're standoffish with strangers. But they're extremely loyal. From my neighborhood, though, it wouldn't take me more than an hour to drive up to Eternal."

"I have a three-legged golden retriever who'd be interested in that Akita, too. She likes playmates."

"Just like me."

"I promise even to be human if I can get home where my life's not on the line. At this point, I just want to get off this ship—it's giving me the creeps."

"Both your incidents took place off the ship, though. I was frankly feeling more secure about you onboard here. Although I'm still curious about Jack Marquez."

"You hadn't seemed all that interested in the Marquezes—but Sara did have a relationship with Willie Bob, and I'm not sure how far it went."

"I'm interested in everyone at this point, Ruby. I'm ruling nothing out."

"Me, either. Not only am I feeling claustrophobic, I'm also feeling more nervous."

"Maybe this will help."

There's a lifeboat fastened to the rail beside us. He reaches inside it and pulls out a bottle of wine.

"I stashed this away for us," he says. "It might be a good Riesling. Then again, it might not. I bought it in town— at least it didn't come from the ship's stock."

"Neat. Of course, if you'd bought it here, you could screw off the cap. Are you planning to break off the cork on the side of the rail?"

"For your information, I planned this." He reaches into his pocket and brings out a Swiss Army knife with a corkscrew.

"I'm impressed, Levinger. You thought of everything."

"Except glasses. I forgot. We'll have to swig from the bottle."

"Do I get first swig?"

"Absolutely. Who says I don't have manners?"

"Hey, it's very good. I'd even go so far as to say it's excellent."

"You're so used to the swill here, you'd like anything I produced. But yeah, it is good."

We take turns silently, even seriously, passing the bottle back and forth until we've polished off at least half of it.

"I guess we were thirsty," I say finally.

"Hungry, too. I didn't eat that dinner."

"Me, either. I figure I can live on crackers for twenty-four hours and enjoy a real meal when we're on land."

"So where are the crackers?"

"I didn't bring any. Sorry."

We're both slightly off-balance for a minute as the wine hits.

"Oh, wait," I blurt out, "we'd better have one meal tomorrow. There's no telling how long we'll be held on the ship."

"Why?"

"Huh?"

"Why will we be held on the ship?"

I sit there for a while and think about that last question. I hadn't decided yet whether to tell Ed about the police coming aboard. I guess it's too late now, unless I can bluff it.

"Just the usual procedures—doesn't that take a long time?"

"Yes, but not more than a few hours—they've allowed for all that, and we'll still be out of here by ten, I'll bet. I was going to ask if you wanted to have a late dinner at one of the good restaurants in Galveston. So what did you mean about being held here?"

"Nothing."

Too bad I'm not sharp right now. I could finesse him any day.

"Did you forget I make my living noticing what people don't say?"

"This isn't very romantic, is it?"

"I had a few plans along that line, too, Ruby. What are you hiding?"

I cave.

"The autopsy showed that Willie Bob didn't have a heart attack. He was killed with a substance that imitated the symptoms. Someone in that embarkation hall murdered him."

"Who knows?"

"Just the police on the mainland. And me. And now you."

"So they're planning to board ship and question everybody? They'll have to let them know in advance."

"No, they won't. They're going to hold everyone with no warning—the police thought it better not to communicate through channels onboard. They don't know who they're dealing with."

"You can say that again."

"Do you?"

"Do I what?"

"Know who they're dealing with."

"I've traced as much as I can, but no, I don't know the extent of it. Not at all. I wish I'd had a few more days."

"I've told you all this. Why can't you fill me in on the rest?"

"I promise you I'll tell you everything I know in the next couple of days. What I'm afraid of now is that the police will board before anything gels, people will be tipped, and they won't get what they're looking for."

"All they're planning to do is to ask questions. I doubt if they're going to hold the whole ship more than a few hours. But I'm sure it'll be into the early hours of the morning, don't you?"

"Yeah."

I've lost his attention now—he seems totally preoccupied with what I've told him. Suddenly he comes back to life again.

"Ruby, you're not planning to tell anyone else, are you?"

"No. I'm sorry I blurted it out to you, Ed. I don't think anyone should know."

"If one person more gets an inkling that you have information, Ruby, you could be in much greater danger than you've been in so far. Do you realize that?"

"Well, it might also depend upon whom you inform, right? You could go on shore right now if you wanted to."

"In case you haven't noticed, we've lifted anchor

already. We're sailing tonight. Tomorrow we'll be at sea all day until we reach home port. I'm not telling anyone."

"You're not investigating this alone. You mean you won't say anything to the people helping you?"

"That's what I'm saying."

"Okay, then—I'll try to relax. We have less than twenty-four hours before we're home. And that includes sleep time."

"With your cabin locked. Unless you'll feel safer at my place."

With his eyes on me again and that half-teasing flicker of a smile, it's tempting.

But I'll wait.

36

When I awake, I have an awful headache and I'm ravenous. But before I let myself think about the long and possibly unpleasant day ahead, I lie in bed for a few minutes. Those soft and not so soft kisses inside my doorway last night are going to have to last a while.

I can't see any of this business going away so fast, and I can imagine Lieutenant Paul Lundy and his colleagues hounding me for the next couple of weeks. Not to mention all the work I have to catch up on. Besides my computer clients, Milt will expect me to do my usual bookkeeping and ordering chores, since he's leaving all the paperwork for me these days. The worst thing about a vacation is having to work double to catch up the first week home—not that this cruise has been anything approaching restful. Although it has had its compensations.

As if by ESP, the phone rings.

"Am I calling too early?"

"Not at all—I was just lying here being lazy."

"I wanted to make sure you were okay—I dropped by a couple of times during the night, but all was quiet."

"I slept the whole night—obviously, you didn't. You were wandering the halls that late?"

"Yeah, I guess so. I came back to the cabin around five, and fell asleep until now. I was going to ask if you wanted to have breakfast, but I really should do some work now that it's late. I still have a couple of leads to check out."

"That's all right. You must feel totally unfinished."

"I'd rather not go over that on the phone, but I'll be looking for you later. I'm glad you had a good night's sleep—I was worried about you."

"I'll miss you at breakfast."

"Me, too. 'Bye."

If Ed's so paranoid he doesn't even trust my blurting out something over the ship's phone system, things must really be getting hairy. I wish today were over.

My head hurts when I move, and I even find myself looking forward to a cup of *Bargain II* coffee. It might taste like swill, but at least it's full of caffeine.

Kevin's going into the dining room as I get there, and

we grab a table for two. I can't take the whole group this early in the morning, but I'm just as glad not to sit by myself today. I don't want to think too much.

"We were looking for you last night, Ruby. We had a Star of David get-together after the costume party."

"Sorry I missed it."

"Were you with your new boyfriend?"

"I was with Ed, but I wouldn't call him my boyfriend, Kevin."

"I would. Essie Sue says you don't know that much about him—just like me with Angel last year."

"It's none of her business, but in any case, I don't have to know that much about him at this point—we're just getting to know each other, not getting engaged like you and Angel did."

"So you like him better than the captain?"

"You've got to be joking."

"The captain's supposed to be a real catch—I have it on good authority."

"I'll save today's catch for the dinner menu. All I want to do now is get back home."

"What are you having for breakfast?"

I get a chance to think about it while Kevin's ordering from the waiter. He's having Mock Lox and Eggs, whatever that is. I'm surprised they even mentioned the lox was imitation. And does that mean the eggs are, too? I'm sick of boxed cereal, but I don't dare try the eggs.

"I'll take some dry toast with jelly on the side, and lots of coffee."

"We're out of bread. This is the last day," the waiter says, as if that's supposed to be self-explanatory.

"I'm just curious. What are you not out of in the way of staples?"

"Well, we have quite a few large cans of beans on hand, and we have a barrel of apples."

"Any barrels of rum?"

He's not amused. "This is breakfast," he says.

"Do you have any more crackers?"

"A few."

"I'll take all of them." The heck with the other passengers—this will get me through the day. "And an apple and coffee."

When Kevin's lox comes, I prefer to look the other way.

"So what is it?" I say.

"I don't know. I think it's got orange coloring on it—some came off on the eggs. But it's not bad."

I realize I'm much happier having the ingredients unnamed. And when the waiter said a *few* crackers, he meant it. He deposits five packs of two on the tablecloth, along with an apple and a pot of coffee. I consider myself lucky.

The headache's fading with every sip of caffeine, and I'm feeling I can cope now. With what, I don't want to know, but I'm ready. Kevin has finished eating, but I notice that he's getting more and more fidgety.

"Kevin, you're making me nervous. Do you realize you're chewing your napkin? I don't think it's going to obliterate the taste of the eggs."

"I'm worried, Ruby. And I don't want to tell Essie Sue."

"What's the matter?"

"I did something dishonest, or at least it felt that way. And now I might have to compound the dishonesty when we go through Customs."

"How come?"

"Well, remember the other day when we had the scavenger hunt? And I beat Essie Sue?"

"Yes—one tends to remember unusual events like that—she's not easy to outmaneuver."

"That's the problem—I think I maneuvered the situation."

"I appreciate the attack of conscience, Kevin, but it was just a game, and she's always taking advantage of circumstances. Don't worry about it."

"But I don't know what to do now. I can't lie to Customs. And I don't want it to all come out that I won unfairly."

I guess we're going to have to start at the beginning, which was what I was trying to avoid. But now I'm curious.

"Okay, just give it to me as it happened."

"I won the hunt because I found a Palm Pilot quicker than Essie Sue did."

"Yeah, you found it almost immediately, if I recall."

"That was because I already knew where it was. I didn't have to go around knocking on cabin doors and asking for one."

"Because?"

The man is beyond tedious.

"Okay, Ruby, because a while back, I found a Palm Pilot stuck in one of the inside pockets of the professor's backpack. Everyone knew his lecture notes had to be taken from his laptop, but this Palm Pilot was extra, you might say. I'd always wanted to try one, so I thought I'd play with it for the rest of the trip, without having anyone take it away from me."

"I didn't think you knew anything about computers."

"I don't, but these handheld things aren't real computers—they're more like toys. At least, I thought they were until I tried to work this. It has menus and stuff, the same as computers. I haven't figured it out yet, but I grabbed it without even thinking when the scavenger hunt called for a Palm Pilot."

"So what? It sounds legitimate to me—you were asked to find one, and you did. End of story. No one cared where it came from."

"Essie Sue would. She'd say it wasn't fair because I'd been hiding it all along, and it didn't even belong to me."

"Essie Sue could think up something more devious than that in her sleep, Kevin. Forget it."

"If you say so. But what do I do with it now? I can't get the thing to work, and I don't want to declare it to Customs as mine. I could get arrested."

"I've got the perfect solution, Kevin."

"I knew you would."

"Give it to me."

"Why? You don't want to get in trouble, either."

"I'll figure out what to tell Customs, and Essie Sue won't know a thing. You can forget you ever saw it, but only on one condition."

"What?"

"That you swear not to tell a living soul I've got it. I mean that, Kevin. Can you do that?"

"Okay. You deal with it."

We go down to Kevin's cabin and he pulls out the Palm Pilot from under the mattress.

"I felt guilty not telling anyone I had it," he says.

"Well, now you don't have it and you won't have to feel bad anymore."

"I guess I'd better stand by in my room," he says. "The captain said all sorts of orders and directions for the last day are coming through the intercom. We're supposed to fill out the evaluation forms, leave our tips in separate envelopes, listen to see when our deck is supposed to come upstairs for disembarkation tonight, and pay any money we owe. They'll let us go floor by floor."

"We also have to fill out forms to get back into the country, remember."

"Sure. And I have to get my passport back."

"You don't need a passport for this sailing, Kevin—these are the U.S. Virgin Islands."

"Well, I brought one anyway. Just to be on the safe side."

It figures.

He's forgotten all about the Palm Pilot—I put it in the zipper compartment of my waist pack while he's talking.

Maybe this is the reason the laptop didn't provide all the information we hoped—Willie Bob might have inserted an extra layer of security by using the handheld to store the really valuable data.

I have to decide fairly quickly whether to go back to my berth and see what's in here, or whether I should go find Ed. He's busy this morning.

I go back and see for myself.

37

I lock the door from the inside, take off my shoes, and hop on the bed. For one thing, I'm tired from the last day's activities, and for another, there's nowhere else to sit *except* on the bed. I turn on the Palm Pilot and make sure it has enough full battery power, then check the various options. I look at the to-do list, the calendar, and the address list—nothing very interesting. The memo section contains two private entries—you need a password to access them. The expense section is fairly cut and dried, listing the initial plane fare on American Airlines to Houston.

Great. The professor's laptop had references to a password, but no password protection enabled. Now his Palm Pilot has a private area with password enabled, but no hint of the password. I grab my own computer and start going over the documents I copied from Willie Bob's files. Now I understand the reference to the Flight Simulator game.

His notes said: "If something happens, see who controls the Flight Simulator program."

It's the *pilot* who controls that game—it's a training manual for pilots. And also, of course, a reference to his own Palm Pilot. I'm close, but where do I find the password to get me into the private memos? I don't know if they're in the laptop files or the Palm Pilot files. And even if I access those memos, they could just be personal notes, not having anything to do with Willie Bob's death. I don't think he would have gone to all the trouble, though, of referring to the Pilot and something happening if there weren't hidden files somewhere. Just to be on the safe side, since I'm not sure I can easily change the identification section to my own name, I tape one of my business cards to the inside, so anyone who finds this will initially assume it's mine and not Willie Bob's. I stick the little machine into the back pocket of my shorts.

I'd better do some quick packing while I'm working this out in my mind. I have nothing to organize, since I'm coming home with exactly what I started out with. It's amazing how little shopping I did on this trip. I sent a couple of wood carvings I liked to Joshie at college, and brought Milt and Grace some guavaberry liqueur imported from St. Martin's. I just didn't have the patience to ferret out anything for myself. Maybe it's because I've been practically disabled for most of the trip, between being hit on the head and almost drowning.

Okay, I've thrown in everything I own, and it's only taken ten minutes to pack. None of this has helped me decide what to do about recovering that password.

I really need to find Ed.

There's a special feel about this last day—fewer passengers are just wandering around, and the activities seem more purposeful. People are also bumping into one another, in a hurry to get somewhere. In other words, it's just like home.

I have no idea where to start looking for Ed, so I head for a few of the places our temple group hangs out. Near the café I run into Yvonne Copeland—Brother's wife—and Sadie Chernoff. Both have seen Ed Levinger this morning—he'd just dropped by the café. The only problem is that Sadie saw him headed toward the ship's offices, and Yvonne noticed him at the same time going in the direction of the bridge. I thank them and try to ignore the gleam in their eyes that tells me I just produced more grist for the rumor mill.

So, which way shall I try? I walk down to the business offices and see nothing but rooms with computers in them and staff busily typing and filing. Maybe the bridge would be more productive—it is supposed to be the hub of the ship. Although with this captain at the helm, it's probably more like the caboose. It turns out that I don't have to fully explore either of these places—something much more intriguing turns up. Out of the corner of my eye I see one of the passenger elevators—its door is clos-ing. I'm certain that I'm hallucinating, but I could swear I see that damned tan leather briefcase in the hands of the mystery man Ed was meeting the other day. That couldn't be—we're out to sea, and I'm sure he's not one of the passengers. I look at him and he looks back briefly, then resumes staring straight ahead and holding the case with both hands in front of him.

In the movies they watch to see where the elevator lights up before running up or down the stairs to meet it. Since most elevators stop all over the place letting out passengers, this has never seemed like much of a plan to me. I do notice that it's headed up, but I also know I'd never have time to check out all those floors just as he got off. I need to see Ed more than ever.

Just so I won't kick myself later, I make one attempt at following the man on the elevator. He probably wouldn't have taken the elevator for just one floor up, and I'll never be able to make more than two stories in time. So that leaves two floors up from where I am now, and I open the stairwell door and run for it. I'm glad my dog, Oy Vey, and I have been running together by the lake for a few months, because I'm in better shape than I was before. I make it without being too winded, but I have nothing to show for my trouble. He's nowhere around.

This is the casino floor, and even on this last day, there are a few die-hards mindlessly putting quarters in the slots. I look at the faces, just to make sure his isn't one of them. One of the gift shops adjoins the casino, but it's mostly empty—probably because the passengers' bills have already been tallied by today and no one's that interested in paying cash for a lot of this drek. The leftovers are pretty pathetic—calendars with the ship's picture on them, bargain perfumes with scents no one would tolerate, and tee shirts saying *I Sailed with Captain Goldberg*— not exactly bestsellers.

Damn—speak of the devil's least favorite advocate— here's the tee shirt king himself. Just what I need when I'm in a hurry.

"Ruby! I was hoping to see you before you left us. How wonderful that you're browsing among my most treasured souvenirs—what do you think of the likeness? I knew you had that little spark for me."

Oh, geez, now he's going to be convinced I was shopping for these horrors, and I'll never get away.

"Essie Sue told me you had good taste."

"Uh—this being the final day, I really have a lot to take care of, Horatio. Nice seeing you."

"No, no. I insist on giving you a complimentary tee shirt of your very own. I'm hoping it will inspire you to take another voyage with us—hopefully in calmer waters."

You can say that again. Troubled waters doesn't begin to describe this experience—not that I'd ever repeat it in this life.

"Perhaps I could surprise you with a visit to Essie Sue and get to know you away from my official duties, Ruby."

Before he can venture further into what I can guarantee would be very troubled waters, I grab the shirt he's pushing at me, nod my thanks or however he wants to interpret it, and head back through the casino. Now I guess I've lost that other guy for good.

It's almost lunchtime, and if I head down toward the restaurant, maybe I'll see Ed. Or with real luck, the man with the briefcase. I've about pushed my good fortune with stairwells today, so I wait and take one of the elevators.

A big mistake.

38

The scenario plays right out in front of me, and there's nothing I can do about it. I watch the elevator door close, and see two men standing by themselves as I enter the car. They don't belong here—they're wearing jeans and ordinary shirts, but they're simply not passengers. I'd bet my life on this, and I might have to. As I move my hand to push the Open Door button, one of them puts his large hand over mine. Before I can cry out, which obviously wouldn't help anyway, the gift tee shirt I'm holding is jammed into my mouth, over my eyes, and roughly tied at the back. Of course it's navy blue, and of course I can't see a thing.

I feel them tying my ankles together, and sense the elevator stopping.

"Hurry," one says. "Are you sure this is all the way down to the galley floor? We have to tell them we have her."

"I only had enough for the feet," the other says.

One throws something to the other, I guess, and I feel my hands being tied with a different material—it's some sort of scarf or cloth. I keep my hands as wide apart as I dare while he's tying, so my circulation won't be cut off. He's in such a hurry I don't think he's doing much checking. They pull off my waist pack and watch and shove me in a corner.

"Put the out of order sign on the elevator door, and make sure it's closed behind us. And that this thing is stopped for as long as we need it."

"Do you think it's okay this way?"

"Yeah—nobody walks into an out-of-service elevator."

"What're they gonna do with her?"

"They'll wait until the passengers get off."

I hear the door slide shut. It's hard to say whether I feel better or worse with them gone—in one way, I'm safer without them, but in another sense, I'm alone in the dark.

I guess I have one advantage—no one but Ed and I know that the police are boarding the ship tonight before the passengers disembark. Surely they'll check this elevator. Or will they? And how do I know these men won't come back before the police have a chance to board?

I shake my head but it doesn't help—the tee shirt won't budge. I try to sit up but I can't balance enough to do it—I should have paid more attention to strengthening my abs at the gym. The only thing left to concentrate on is my hands, which are twisted behind my back. I'm fortunate that I kept them a bit apart, though, because I have some wiggle room. My guess is that with everything going on this afternoon, no one will do anything about me for a few hours. If I'm lucky.

I lie where I am on my side, try to relax, and start working on the cloth binding my hands. If I can keep moving my wrists around and around, maybe the scarf or whatever will loosen. My hands have always been strong, so I take advantage of that by making fists and pulling them in opposite directions. I feel the binding cutting into my wrists, so I have to be careful not to start any bleeding I won't be able to staunch. I'm getting nowhere, so I go into high-intensity intervals. I pull as hard as I can and wriggle at the same time, then I stop entirely and rest. Then I start again.

It finally works—the cloth knot loosens enough for me to slip out one of my fists, and with that hand, I pull the binding off the other hand. Yep, my wrists are definitely bleeding—I can feel it when I touch them. I can't seem to untie the tee shirt knot, and maybe it's a good thing. If someone checks on me, I ought to be wearing it. If I put my hands behind me as soon as I hear anything, I'll be able to maintain the same position as when they left. What I want to do now is to pull the shirt down from my eyes and nose, still keeping it available in case I have to pull it up again.

I have no idea how long it's taken me to accomplish this much—it seems as though a long time has passed. I have mixed feelings about knocking on the walls with my arms, since I'm afraid I'll only get the attention of the men who put me here. I guess I'll have to start yelling and bumping if anyone's going to rescue me. My feet are tied firmly with rope, and I seem to be too tired to make anything happen, no matter how hard I try.

Okay, I'm going to make a racket. I bang against the wall of the elevator and call out as hard as I can and still keep part of the tee shirt covering my mouth in case they come back.

Nothing happens. Even the emergency button has been disconnected. The elevator seems almost soundproof. Too bad this is a passenger deck elevator and not the big, glassed-in one that's the showpiece of the center section of the ship.

While I'm rolling around on the floor, I feel the Palm Pilot in my back pocket and take it out to see if it's broken. It has a cover on it, and as far as I can see, it's fine. And most conveniently, these machines are backlit. Too bad it isn't a wireless gizmo, but I'm grateful enough for some light in the room, even though it's eerily green from the LCD screen. I push myself up with my back to the wall for support, and sit with my bound feet out in front of me. I have either all the time in the world, or no time at all, to search this Palm Pilot for secrets. I have it only because I

didn't put it in my waist pack, so maybe it's here for a purpose. If I can find something that will help me later today,
I'll be ahead of the game. Or not.

It's hard to read the entries with all this sweat running
into my eyes. Besides feeling very hot in this enclosed
space, I guess I'm also nervous, though I'm trying not to
think about that. If I can concentrate on doing something
positive, at least I can fool myself into thinking I'm making
progress, and not just marking time until they come back.

The professor's life, judging from his daily calendar,
wouldn't exactly inspire envy. He was meticulous about
his schedule, though—he even lists his daily walks and the
number of miles. I see no reference to a family or to any
activities with other people. He seems to have spent his
time writing journal articles, attending occasional con-
ferences, teaching, and walking. No reference to his trips
to the liquor store, I notice.

I've searched every entry in this machine, and I can't
find any clue to a password. Maybe all that information is
in the laptop, which of course is now inaccessible to me.
I'm thinking about his scrupulous attention to detail in his
daily schedule, and something keeps nagging at me. That
expense ledger seems awfully sparse. A stickler like this
guy would certainly have noted his food expenses on the
way to the port, and not just the price of the airline ticket.
And there's a calendar listing of other business trips in the
past few months, but no entries for those trips under the
expense register. Of course it's possible that he just hadn't
gotten around to entering those figures, but the behavior

doesn't fit, characterwise. I'd expect a complete listing of all trips and expenses.

What *does* fit about this lone entry is the fact that it concerns a flight, and that conforms with the original clue about the Flight Simulator game and the pilot controlling it. I try the one expense entry as a password. First, I put in the numbers themselves—the price of the ticket, then the date of the entry—but these numbers don't work. I try *Houston* and *Galveston*—no good. Then I try *airlines,* and finally *American.* Bingo.

Well, at least his clues were consistent—all related to flight, with *American* being the password into the private area. I'm proud of myself. Too bad my little ego boost happens to be taking place at the same time my feet are tied in ropes and I'm waiting for killers to come to my rescue. Unless Ed gets here first. In my dreams.

My hands are shaking as I try to log into the Palm Pilot system with the password. They *should* be shaking—not only don't I know what I'm about to see, but I have limited time in which to see it, since the battery power from these little AAAs will last only so long. The one good thing about this is that if someone down the line takes this handheld from me, he or she won't be able to turn it on right away without changing the batteries.

What I find surprises me. The first entry is a list of dates, times, and precise locations of illegal dumping activities from the *Bargain II.* Professor Gonzales even records names of witnesses to the dumping of waste products, adding that:

Additional evidence has emerged concerning the trans-
portation of toxic waste canisters from the mainland U.S.,
separate and apart from the ship's own refuse.

He adds a chilling note:

We are close, perhaps dangerously close, to discovering the
hierarchy of this organization. This next voyage in particu-
lar should be critical to our findings.

Illegal dumping—who'd have thunk it? Willie Bob
Gonzales has turned out to be a most complex hombre—
historical researcher, imbibing clown, loner, and pene-
trating undercover operative. Unfortunately, also dead.

I've read that illegal dumping has resulted in huge fines
for shipping companies in the past, but in this particular
case, it's led to murder as well—in part, I suppose,
because of the risky business the *Bargain II* picked up on
the side. It's also possible that the professor was a part of
the plot, and was killed by his confederates for some
reason.

I don't know whether to stop reading and start banging on the walls again, or to keep going—there's one
more private entry to check. The men who tied me up
aren't planning to be back until after the passengers are
scheduled to disembark. Of course, they don't know
about the police boarding, but who knows exactly when
that will be? I'm also hoping my traveling companions
might miss me by that time, and start looking for me. And

on the pessimistic side, my captors might need the elevator so badly for disembarkation that they'll come and move me to an even more secluded location.

Sounds as though I've already made my decision—I'll keep searching the private sections. There's one more entry, and I access it using the password *American*.

I'm sorry I found this one. Not that it can't be explained in a nonfrightening manner, but because there are other interpretations, too. It's a sparse list, consisting of only two names. The first:

Jack Marquez.

Odd, because he's already referred to an appointment with Jack and Sara in his laptop notes. Why would Jack's name be a part of his most private files? Was Willie Bob blackmailing him? Or was Jack after *him* in some way? Was Jack part of the hierarchy he referred to?

The last name could also mean almost anything. That's why it numbs me:

Ed Levinger.

39

Okay, don't panic. Not easy to say in my present position, with legs that feel like logs, not to mention the bleeding wrists. The question is—if Ed finds me, is that good news or bad? Chances are, it's good. Waste dumping is no doubt the huge story Ed's been tracking, and the professor was working with him. On the other hand, who's more mobile than a journalist? Writing an article could be great cover for something nasty, and as yet, Ed's revealed nothing to me about what he's really doing. Maybe he and Jack are in this together, and Willie Bob found out. Of course the reality is—I know next to nothing, and this is all just speculation.

While I'm speculating, I might as well kick walls. I restore the privacy code to the two files, close the top of the Palm Pilot, and put it away in my back pocket. I sit on the cloth that was used to tie my hands, just in case the wrong people come in to check on the noise. I also adjust the tee shirt on my face so that I can pull it up at a moment's notice. According to the clock on the Palm Pilot, I've been in here for a couple of hours. Needless to say, it seems like eons, and with the air circulation shut off, the tropical heat in here has the whammy of a blow-torch.

I've exhausted myself and begin nodding off when I hear a faint sound. Since this elevator is practically sound-proof, the source must be a lot closer than it appears to be. I pull the tee shirt the rest of the way over my face, making sure that this time, I have more breathing space. And of course I don't have that big bunch of cloth stuffed in my mouth anymore.

Since I can't see, I'm hoping someone will call out my name, but I'm disappointed. The door opens and people are here, but they aren't friends. In fact, they smell like the same unsavory, and I do mean unsavory, characters who brought me here. One or both of them chews tobacco, and that lovely scent mingles with great quanti-ties of stale sweat to produce an unfortunately memo-rable signature. They say nothing—just lift me—one grabbing my feet and the other reaching under my arms from behind. They don't seem to notice or care that the scarf binding my hands is missing. I decide not to cry out, even though I got rid of the mouth muffler—they'd just stuff in part of the tee shirt again, and they could knock out my teeth in the process.

They dump me into some kind of container with rollers on it, like a laundry or cleaning cart, I guess. Then they throw a tarp over my head and start the elevator again. I notice it doesn't stop from floor to floor—we go up for what seems an interminable time, but probably isn't more than a few seconds, until we reach our destination. They roll me for a few feet, open a door, and push the cart inside.

The first thing I feel is blessed air-conditioning—it's almost worth being exposed to the unknown, but not quite. There's also a kind of sweetish odor in here, acrid, too, and familiar. It even overpowers the fragrance of the pungent pair who delivered me, and that's not an easy feat—unless they've slipped away already. I wait a few minutes, and still hear nothing. At last I decide there's no one in this room. I gently lower the tee shirt from my eyes to look around.

As I lift up the tarp, three things happen in sequence, making this whole experience surreal. First, I instantly recognize my surroundings. I realize next that this is a good time to let out a piercing shriek, since the room is not soundproof. And last, I come face-to-face with my abductor, who, at the sound of the scream, comes rushing into the room with his toupee askew.

Only this time, it's not funny.

40

Captain Goldberg is not amused.

"They told me you were gagged and bound," he says, the simper gone from his manner and the stupidity gone from his eyes. "Fools."

I try to scream again, and I bite him as he stuffs the shirt back into my mouth. With my arms free, I aim for his eyes with my forefingers. None of this works—the shirt gets stuffed in, and he dodges my jabs. He holds my painful wrists with one hand and reaches for a phone with the other. Within seconds, two different men are back in the room, tying my arms behind me.

"Secure her mouth and leave her eyes free," he orders.

I slump back into the cart while the captain goes into the bathroom to take care of his bite. When he comes back, wearing a bandage, he has the men sit me up straight and then stand guard by the doorway.

"You foolish, foolish woman," he says. "I'd like to talk to you, but you've made that impossible."

I nod my head over and over, pointing it toward the water pitcher on his desk.

"Do you want water? My men can stuff your mouth again at the first hint of a sound," he says.

I nod yes.

I hope this is a deal, because I'm dying for some water, and I'm curious myself about what he'll say to me. I guess he's curious, too.

He lets one of the men slowly raise the cloth binding my mouth, and takes out the gag.

"Cover her," Horatio says to the other man, who reaches into his pocket to grip what I'm sure is a gun. I get the message.

To my surprise, he hands one of the men a new pint-sized bottle of water and lets him feed me almost the whole thing. I'm beyond grateful—not that I'll let him know. The water puts me into some sort of soporific state—it feels *so* good. Part of me just wants to sit here in the air-conditioning and fade out, but unfortunately, I'm a realist.

"I'm sure someone heard me call out," I tell him, "and I'm also sure they're looking for me."

"And I suppose you're wondering why I've had you

brought to my quarters, too? You need to know that on this ship, these quarters are sacrosanct. No one enters the captain's quarters without permission."

Same ol', same ol'—the man might not be playing the fool anymore, but he's still a prig. I also realize he's probably right—no one will know I'm here if he wants to hide me in one of these bedrooms. With only two entrances, these quarters are a lot more secure than the elevator was. Still, I might as well find out as much as I can. I'm not encouraging him to untie my arms and legs—first, because I don't think he will, but also because I don't want anyone frisking me and finding the Palm Pilot, even if it is password-protected. With any attention at all, he'd see it belonged to the professor.

I'll get straight to the point before he takes control of the conversation.

"You had me knocked over the head once," I say, "and tried to have me killed the second time, so are you planning to finish the job now?"

"In good time," he says, "when we have the ship to ourselves. And perhaps if you tell me all you know, you'll be let go."

Oh, right. That was a pathetic tag line if I ever heard one. I guess I'm supposed to be reassured.

"If you want to redeem yourself, Ruby, start at the beginning and tell me why you were snooping."

Redeem myself? Always sanctimonious.

"Okay, I'll tell you exactly what happened. I was trying to take a shot of the temple, and if your thugs reported to you correctly, you'll understand that I took the picture by reaching over my head. The photo didn't even come out, and you already know I couldn't see anything directly. So that's the prelude to my getting knocked in the head and having my compact memory flash card stolen. Only you didn't stop there—you tried to get rid of me for good on the island. What's so important you want to kill me for it?"

I'm glad I already know the answer to that, thanks to Willie Bob. My main goal right now is to keep expounding my innocence and not give away my two aces—that I know Willie Bob was murdered and that the police are boarding ship tonight. If I can just keep myself alive until then, maybe I'll have a chance. Another thing   why isn't Ed looking for me? Assuming Horatio killed Willie Bob for discovering the dumping scheme, can I also assume he doesn't know Ed is investigating, too? Or maybe Ed isn't even on to this angle—I haven't had a chance to ask him about it.

"We think you've discovered something that's better kept secret—that's why you're here now. As for my being responsible for your being hit on the head or almost drowning, you're wrong."

"Well, if you're so innocent, why involve yourself now? I don't know anything, so let me go. Trust me, I just want to go home—you'll never hear from me again."

"You know more than you're saying, Ruby. You've recognized somebody you shouldn't have."

"I have no idea what you're talking about."

I'm not about to enlighten him. It's clear that he hasn't a clue as to what I know or don't know. But he has somehow found out that I followed that man with the briefcase when he rode up the elevator at noon today. The guy must have seen me dash from the stairwell door when I ran up the stairs trying to outrace his elevator. Maybe he was already hidden in one of the rooms off the corridor, but he saw me. That's why they captured me. He told the captain, who then found me in the gift shop on the casino floor. Once he saw who I was, he ordered his men to grab me. If only I'd looked when that elevator door opened.

No time to cry over that.

"Do you want me to use this cart as a bathroom? I've been tied up for hours."

He's cool, but even he can't stop a wince at that possibility—I know the type.

"Use the bathroom in the second bedroom."

"Wheel her in there," he says to the guys, "and lift her out right at the toilet. Untie her hands and stand at the door—no mistakes."

"How can I go when my ankles are tied?"

"You can balance with your hands untied—take it or leave it."

I take it. Since I'm no Houdini, I don't expect to make a cool getaway out of this maneuver, but it's better than the alternative, and at least I can get some relief.

They let me shut the door, and I do manage to sit down without falling. I go quickly so that I can arrange my clothing and still have time to wash down my bloody wrists under the faucet. When I pull myself up to the sink, one look in the mirror jerks me out of any denial that I'm in the midst of a major ordeal.

Then I have one halfhearted idea. There's a glass on the sink, and I break it, but not to fight my way out of here—with three men in the other room and my feet tied, there's no chance of that.

When one of the men bursts through the door at the sound of the glass shattering, I hold up one of my bloody wrists. For a tough guy, he sure doesn't like the sight of blood.

41

"Hey, you guys! This broad's trying to kill herself."

While the yelling's going on, I hide a big piece of the broken glass in my front shirt pocket. The three men rush the bathroom door at one time, and the scene turns into something out of a Marx brothers flick.

"Put her in the cart. She's not committing suicide— she's just playing for sympathy." In response to his captain's orders, one of the men tosses me back into the handcart. I lie down on my side, with my knees scrunched up fetal-style. I'm hoping they'll forget my untied hands, but the captain strides over to me, ready to bark commands again, or worse. He's interrupted by a phone call.

"All right, I'll come to the bridge right away," he says, and then turns to his men.

"Wheel her to the back bedroom and put a gag in again—I don't want her making a sound. It's time for the captain's Farewell Address on the loudspeaker system. This will all be finished soon."

I'd better talk fast before they gag me again.

"I know he wants you to stand guard outside my door until he gets back," I say. "But before you go, could you let me have some more water?"

"You're kidding, right? After everything you've pulled? Shove it."

Ah, the power of suggestion. I was afraid they'd insist on standing over me until Horatio came back. Now they can't wait to punish me by leaving the room and ignoring me. I'm docile as they gag me again—that's the least of my worries. Besides, I'll be able to pull the gag out whenever I feel like it.

As soon as they close the door I get to work freeing my feet with the large glass shard I'd put in my shirt pocket. The rope's tough, but the piece of glass is sharp as a knife, and it's cutting through, bit by bit. Despite the air-conditioning in these rooms, I'm soaking wet just from the stress of trying to slash this rope before Horatio comes back. I needn't worry about being surprised, though, because I can hear his speech over the amplifier all the way in this back room. You'd think this was a State of the Union address:

> *"My Dear Passengers, this is your captain speaking. It is now ten P.M. We've had a glorious cruise and are now about to enter the Port of Galveston, where we disembark. The* Bargain II *will now take its place as the most memorable experience of your life, and as its captain, I stand humbly on its decks to claim a place in your heart. Please listen carefully as our communications officer gives you important instructions about the procedures for forming lines to leave the ship.*
>
> *Wait—one more announcement. I've been asked by the Temple Rita contingent to ask Ms. Ruby Rothman to please join her group for the disembarkation process."*

Nice touch. The good news is that they *are* looking for me, after all. Ed must know I'm in trouble if I didn't show up for lunch or dinner, and I guess Essie Sue was the one who asked for the announcement. The bad news is that Horatio's not giving a long sermon after all—I didn't expect that quick turnover to the communications officer, which can only mean he's on his way back here.

I cut as fast as I can into this thick rope, and finally it snaps. I push it under me, and then I throw the tarp over the bottom half of my body like a blanket, and make sure it covers up my hands, too. I'm sure they won't know the difference, and at least my free limbs won't be out there for all to see. To get ready for anything, I keep the shard in my right hand, and wiggle my numb legs to get the circulation back. I'm as ready as I'll ever be, though for what, I'm not sure.

I don't have to wait long. I hear Horatio come in and shut the door behind him.

"Where is she?"

"She's where you told us to put her, Captain—in the back bedroom with her gag in. You don't hear her, do you?"

"Have you been checking on her?"

"Yes," they lie.

All my muscles tighten as I hear Horatio open my door. I now have a plan, but who knows if I can carry it out?

As he opens the door, a big squawk comes from the loudspeaker.

Attention. This is Lieutenant Sandor with the Galveston police. The police have boarded the Bargain II *and ask for your complete cooperation so that you will be able to leave the ship with as brief a delay as possible. Remain in line until we give you further instructions. Thank you.*

I can't see Horatio in my scrunched-down position, but I feel the tension as I hear him audibly draw in a breath. He's surprised, all right—I was afraid the police raid might have been leaked once we docked, but it's obvious he didn't know.

I hear him running back into the other room.

"Get out of here," he says to the men. "Use the other

exit from my bedroom—it goes to the corridor. You can't be seen in the captain's quarters."

Why—because they look like thugs? Or because they *are* thugs and have criminal records? It's a bit clearer when I hear him say, "As captain, I'll have to receive the police in these quarters. Get down to the deck and stand by with your pagers."

"But what are you going to do with *her*? We can wheel her below."

"She's secure, and they're on their way—I can't risk having them see you rolling something out of my quarters, when I'm not even sure what the police are here for. Go!"

Horatio's back to me in a flash, and I try to lift my head so he won't peel back the other end of the tarp and expose my unbound feet. He buys that, and peeks under the tarp—my mouth is neatly gagged, my eyes are covered again with the tee shirt, and the shard of glass is stowed away in my fist. He turns to wheel me into the bedroom closet, when I hear banging on the door in the other room.

"Captain Goldberg?"

The police come into the outer room without waiting for an answer.

"Captain," they call as they enter, "are you there? We need to establish some procedures for questioning the passengers before they disembark."

"One moment, gentlemen," I hear him say. "Please state your purpose and I'll be glad to cooperate."

I hear him walk toward the room where the police are, having to abandon the cart in the middle of the back bedroom, with me still in it. I take this opportunity to give out a shrieking *geshrei,* but I make a mistake in my timing. I should have lifted my head from the tarp first to make sure he was safely in the other room, but hey, who thinks that clearly?

As I scream, *"Help, he's got me in here,"* and leap out of the cart, Horatio panics. He turns back toward the cart and does a choke hold on me with one arm before I can defend myself with the piece of glass. With his other hand, he reaches into his jacket pocket for a gun.

Two policemen rush into the bedroom, but stop short. "He's got a gun, lady!"

Yeah, I can see that—he's waving it around in front of my eyes.

Horatio's regaining some of his composure now. He realizes, I guess, that he's lost his chance of playing the innocent captain anymore. He straightens up and begins to walk me past them, and out of the bedroom.

As we head into the main room, he motions for the other police officers to move out of the way. What he doesn't count on, though, is the main door to his quarters opening once again.

It's Essie Sue, with Ed right behind her.

She doesn't seem to be aware of the gun at my head—that figures. When Essie Sue has her mind on something concerning her own welfare, which is most of the time, such trivialities escape her notice.

"Cousin Horatio, quit clowning around with Ruby—
this is no time for romance. I want a complete account of
why my group hasn't been allowed to leave the ship. I told
the police we had a protector in the highest echelons
here, but that didn't seem to impress them. You have a lot
of explaining to do."

Yes! Just the break I needed. The captain is so flum-
moxed by the walking non sequitur who's just entered the
room that he's thrown off his stride. The gun wavers, and
I slash at Horatio's arm with the glass shard. I swivel and
duck out of his way. But are the police ready to shoot the
gun out of his hand now that I'm at a distance? No—
they're still gawking at Essie Sue.

Ed's the only one besides me who takes advantage of
the captain's momentary hesitation—he runs toward
Horatio and flings himself at him, trying to deflect his
weapon and knock him down. It would have worked if the
gun hadn't gone off.

All I can see is a gaggle of men thrashing around. The
police have emerged from the trance Essie Sue put them
in, and they head toward me to give me cover. Horatio,
meanwhile, seems energized now that his gun's gone off,
and he keeps shooting. He backs out the door, pushing
Essie Sue in front of him for protection, and then disappears. He doesn't take her with him as a hostage, I notice.
Smart man—that might save his life, but it would be a life
not worth living.

I lie on the floor, relieved to be alive, though I look like
something from the sea that the sharks rejected. All my

bloody wounds are oozing, and I haven't eaten for about fourteen hours, but I'm thankful it's not worse. It takes a few seconds before I sit up, suddenly realizing that this nightmare is far from over. Horatio is gone—maybe even off shooting someone else, though I suspect he's run out of bullets by now. The police are on their intercoms, or cell phones, or whatever, calling for backup in the chase for the captain.

Essie Sue is sitting on the floor by me. She has been rendered speechless—a once-in-a-lifetime experience. I guess she finally understood that her cousin had been brandishing a gun, not his love object. Although who knows what she thinks—I'm sure, like all of us, she's still in shock from the last few seconds. I doubt that this whole sequence of events, starting with the police entry, lasted more than five minutes. It just *seems* like an eternity.

I suddenly see the police circling around someone else on the floor. Oh, God, it's Ed, and unlike Essie Sue and me, he's not getting up.

"It's only a shoulder wound, lady."

One of the policemen is holding a cloth to stifle the blood flow, and I try unsuccessfully to cradle Ed's head in my lap.

"Leave it to us, ma'am. He might have other injuries. The paramedics will be here soon."

I crawl directly over him this time, to look in his eyes. "Is he unconscious?"

"No," Ed says. He even manages to turn up a corner of his mouth in a vain attempt at a grin.

"Are you hurting?" Stupid question, but considering the state I'm in, it's all I can get out.

"I wouldn't want to go dancing, but I'm fine. Are you okay?"

"A lot better than you. I was able to jump out of that maniac's way."

"What's the deal?" he says. "Every time I try to save you, you've already saved yourself. Keep this up and I'll have to join men's lib to get some self-esteem."

I bend down and kiss him. "Your self-esteem is in no danger of being deflated in this life."

"Here's to my not suffering any other deflations," he says.

"I'll be the judge of that."

Essie Sue's state of shock is wearing off. "Give the man some air, Ruby. The ambulance people are in the corridor—I can hear them."

If that's true, they've had to fight their way through whatever commotion her cousin is still causing out there. But happily, the captain's not my problem anymore—the police can handle him. I get up to make room for the stretcher and the emergency team.

"I'm coming with you," I tell Ed.

"Good. Just promise you won't make me talk."

"Not on your life. Why do you think I'm coming along?"

While Ed's being examined, I tag the lead cop to get an update on the captain's whereabouts. I'm not at all sure how safe this EMT team's going to be if Horatio's still on the loose.

"What's happening out there? Don't you think you'd better check before you take this man away?"

"It's quiet. The passengers are still lined up, and Captain Goldberg seems to have disappeared."

"You mean he jumped ship?"

"No, we've watched the waters around the ship. We think he's still aboard. The exits are closed and no one's getting off."

"So how do we know he won't shoot at the stretcher?"

"It's unlikely. He won't want to give himself away, and we think he'll try to hide and wait it out."

"He's not the only one on board who's involved in this scheme, you know."

"We've been filled in, ma'am. No one's getting off the liner. Including you people here."

"But I'm going with Mr. Levinger."

"No, ma'am, you're not. You'll have to wait here in the room. It's a lot better than waiting in those lines outside."

I see I can't move this guy. "Okay, but can't you get Ed out some other way?"

"Already taken care of. We're lowering him to a police medic's launch—it's tied up at the side of the ship away from the pier. Just let us do our job."

I don't like the idea of lowering him, but I leave it to the experts—I hope they know what they're doing.

The stretcher team is already taking Ed out the door— all I can do is wave, since I'm not allowed to leave the room. He waves back and gives me a thumbs-up.

"Take care," he says.

Oy—I should be telling *him* that.

Several of the cops leave, since the leftovers in this

room don't constitute much of a threat to the public safety. One lone guy is assigned to stay and guard us. I'm wondering just how many hours I'm going to be stuck in this room with Essie Sue, when Kevin comes through the door from the corridor.

"I talked my way up here," he says. "Someone said Essie Sue was headed this way. Where is she?"

"Over there on the floor," I say. "Go speak to her. She'll fill you in on what you missed."

"I missed something? I'm always left out of the activities, Ruby—it's not fair. You probably know why the police boarded the ship, and I'm the last to hear the news. Maybe they know I stole the professor's Palm Pilot. I decided to come ask Essie Sue what I should do."

So much for his vow of silence.

"Did you tell anybody in authority that you gave it to me?"

"No, I told you I was still looking for the right authority—that's why I hunted down Essie Sue."

Well, I guess he knows authority when he sees it.

"For your information, Kevin, you're probably a lot safer up here. The police are looking for our esteemed captain, who just shot his way out of here, almost taking his cousin as a hostage. He shot Ed Levinger in the shoulder, and Horatio's still at large somewhere on the ship."

"See? I told you I always miss everything. You guys leave me out."

I'd say this was pretty riveting news, but nothing seems to have sunk in except the fact that Kevin was out of the loop. So what else is new? Me, Incorporated, is still his wholly owned enterprise.

"You really ought to talk with Essie Sue, Kevin—she's been through a lot tonight."

As if I haven't. Anything to get rid of Kevin for a few minutes so I can beg my way out of here. I don't think Ed's wound is serious, but who knows what complications could develop? I'll feel better if I'm there at the emergency room. Besides, he still owes me answers—lots of them. I don't even know if he had a lead on the captain's involvement in all this.

Uh-oh. Either Kevin has finally gotten on Essie Sue's nerves or vice versa—they're over in the corner arguing.

"Don't be ridiculous, Rabbi. Can't you see that my cousin is obviously deeply disturbed? My family doesn't produce criminals."

"I don't care. He promised me."

"The man is running from the police—this is no time to collect souvenirs." Essie Sue is up off the floor and pacing furiously, with Kevin following her in circles.

I know I'll hate myself for this, but now I'm curious. I should stay a million miles away, but I go over to check it out.

"What's up?"

"Nothing, Ruby—absolutely nothing." Essie Sue glances at Kevin with a look usually reserved for me. "Rabbi, don't cross me. You'd be better off planning your remarks for the Welcome Home party I've organized at the airport when we fly back to Austin."

"But he gave his word."

"The rabbi wants to benefit from one of my cousin's generous impulses, Ruby, and I feel it's not timely or seemly."

"Fair is fair, Essie Sue." Kevin keeps at it. "Horatio told me he'd give me one of his used captain's hats to take home as a souvenir of the cruise. This is my last chance to get it before we leave. If he is a gangster, he certainly won't need it in prison. Besides, it's only an old one—he has lots more."

"He's not a gangster, you idiot. Can't you see this kind of talk could ruin my family's distinguished legacy?" Kevin might have done it now—Essie Sue's legacy is not to be taken lightly—in fact, the heavier the better. The temple is still raising money to erect the five-thousand-pound marble statue memorializing Essie Sue's sister.

"What do you think, Ruby?"

"I'd say don't look a legacy in the mouth if you know what's good for you, but I'm staying out of it."

"Tough. I'm getting my hat. He promised."

Kevin marches into the captain's bedroom before Essie Sue has a chance to curse him out again, and heads for the clothes closet. It'll serve him right if one of Horatio's toupees is still in the hat.

The next thing we hear is a yell.

"Help, police—it's him!"

Our one guard runs into the bedroom with his gun drawn, and Kevin rushes right past him into my arms, almost knocking me down.

"Give it up," the policeman says. "Drop the weapon."

Horatio's in his own closet. He's just standing there, gun down at his side and no rug on his head. After he ran out of the room earlier, he must have ducked back through the door from the corridor to his bedroom. Clever, I'd say. Since we were all in the main room or the back bedroom, no one had a reason to look for him there.

"But he's got a gun," I yell to the policeman. "Cover yourself."

"Nah. If he had any more bullets, he'd have fired some shots to get out of here."

"Or grabbed Kevin," I add.

"No, Ruby, he didn't have a chance to do that—I ran away as soon as I saw him."

"Don't shoot—I'll come out," Horatio says. "This is all a big mistake."

Tell me about it.

"See, Ruby—you heard the captain—this has all been a mistake," Essie Sue says.

"Don't try to shoot yourself, Horatio," she calls out. "I've got a great lawyer."

43

E-mail from: Nan
To: Ruby
Subject: *Hot Pastramis—and I Do Mean Hot*

You have no idea how relieved I was to get your call, telling me you were safe and sound in Eternal, and I can imagine how long it's going to take to get back in decent physical condition after your ordeal on the ship. Please, Ruby, take it easy, but get back on-line fast—I want to hear everything.

Just in case you missed it, I'm scanning in an article Paul Lundy sent me from the pages of your local newspaper, the *Eternal Ear*. It came out on the weekend you were getting checked out medically and debriefed by the police. Although it's not news to *you,* I still thought you'd appreciate seeing it in print:

Authorities Investigate Hot Pastramis and Quell Riot at Airport

The meticulously planned Welcome Home party to greet a contingent of Eternal citizens returning from a Caribbean cruise vacation was rudely interrupted yesterday when a group of congregants from Eternal's Temple Rita rioted at the airport. They and their loved ones had been the recipients of ten whole pastramis ordered as door prizes in a lottery conducted by Mrs. Essie Sue Margolis in her capacity as fundraising Chair of the congregation. Apparently, the pastramis, bought at one fourth the usual wholesale price, turned up reported as stolen goods during a Customs investigation at the Mexican border. They had already been delivered to family members of the lottery winners, several of whom became deathly ill but later recovered.

The congregants were also assessed

heavy fines and faced possible indictment, producing the totally understandable reaction at the air- port upon Mrs. Margolis's return. Mrs. Margolis stated:

"The pastramis were guaranteed to be hot, but certainly not hot. The Margolis name would never be connected with anything criminal—I was told the pastramis were a bar- gain, and I grabbed them. Since when has saving money been illegal? I'm countersuing the government. That's all I have to say until I talk to my lawyer."

E-mail from: Ruby
To: Nan
Subject: *If This Is Winning, What's Losing?*

So much for my prize vacation. Although look what could have happened if I'd come in second—food poisoning! Essie Sue still can't believe criminality runs in her genes, but I notice she doesn't defend Horatio in my presence anymore.

Thanks again for being my backup and getting me in touch with all the right people when I was out of the country.

Ed's back in San Antonio and doing well. I was furious because the Galveston police wouldn't let me visit him in the hospital that last night. Instead, they questioned our whole group and then herded us into a bus to the Houston air-port in the wee hours of the morning. We were able to catch a fairly empty 6 A.M. flight home, but Ed was stuck at the hospital for another day, filling in the police.

More later. Ed's on the phone.

E-mail from: Nan
To: Ruby
Subject: *Details*

It's later—are you still on the phone?

E-mail from: Ruby
To: Nan
Subject: *I'm Back*

Here's the rest of the story. A year or so ago, Ed was doing a profile of some local business hotshots for his paper. One of them owned a cruise line, and Ed ran into a source who was sure the line was doing some heavy-duty illegal dump-ing. The story sounded sexy and had a local connection, and the paper let him run with it.

An early cruise led him to Willie Bob Gonzales, who lectured for the line, was an old-style environmentalist, and was horrified when he discovered on his own that someone was dumping canisters of toxins into deep water. He agreed to work with Ed, and the rest is history—that is, *he*'s now history.

Horatio was a part-owner of the financially sinking ship, and the toxic waste deal was a lifesaver for him. The operation involved really big money—enough, even, that he could pay people to attempt murder for him. He had a man try to drown me, but he did the original killing—Willie Bob's—all by himself. When Horatio discovered the professor's involvement, he realized he could not only lose the ship but also his precious reputation. He was afraid to delegate this murder, and it turns out he was pretty clever about it. He got rid of the professor in a way that avoided any attention directed to the actual voyage. If he had thrown Willie Bob overboard during the sailing, for example, there could have been witnesses or repercussions. The chaotic embarkation area was a perfect setting.

The captain, wearing a baseball hat and dressed casually like the passengers, avoided Essie Sue and waited until after she had passed the professor over to me. At that moment, when hordes of people were still milling around us, I was trying to deal with the photographer while supporting a pretty smashed Willie Bob. Horatio darted behind the

professor and injected him with potassium chloride, a substance he'd procured
with no trouble from one of his shady
contacts. Blending into the crowd afterward was easy, and Horatio was gone by
the time Willie Bob went down. Within a
few minutes, he was back in his quarters changing into full uniform.

E-mail from: Nan
To: Ruby
Subject: *Questions*

What about *you* and Ed, dummy—he even
saved you at Buck Island. And you
haven't said a word about the phone
call.

E-mail from: Ruby
To: Nan
Subject: *Answers*

Ed didn't save me when I almost drowned,
but he was right there on the spot. One
of the elevator guys confessed to being
part of the crew that day and pushing
my head underwater. Captain's orders, he
said—I knew too much about the payoff
money.
    The man Ed met in the rain that day
when I saw them at the church was a well-

known courier—he was responsible for
leaving the payoff money for the captain. Ed had gotten to know him under the
pretext of initiating some off-color
deal of his own, which, of course, he
never intended to follow up. Ed didn't
suspect the captain until much later—too
late to warn me specifically. He just
knew from the beginning that I was poking around in dangerous waters—pardon
the pun—and wanted me to back off.
Frankly, Ed didn't think Horatio was
smart enough to maneuver the dumping,
and the courier didn't dare open his
mouth about who was involved. The
courier didn't do any of the strong-arm
work. One of the other men confessed to
seeing me as he came to pick up the
briefcase inside the synagogue drop. He
was the guy who knocked me over the head
and stole my camera's memory card.

Willie Bob Gonzales was into a number
of things, and I don't know if they
were all totally legit. I still wonder
if he might have been blackmailing Jack
Marquez about his supposedly Jewish
origins—otherwise, why would Jack's name
have been in the secret section of his
Palm Pilot? If that's true, I don't think
Sara knew, nor do I think I'll ever know.

I guess I'm putting off your question. I think about Ed a lot, and I
liked the phone call. But I still value
my independence.

E-mail from: Nan
To: Ruby
Subject:*P.S.*

You think too much.

44

E-mail from: Ed
To: Ruby
Subject: *Winged*

Thanks for sending me the piece from the *Eternal Ear*—I'm not amused at being scooped on the cruise story by the likes of the Obnoxious One. To get even, I produced my own version—the paper printed it yesterday—the first of three articles. If you can't get the San Antonio paper there, I'll have the office send you one.

When this shoulder starts throbbing in the middle of the night, I'm not at

all sure it's worth it. I guess you know
what I mean—you got pretty banged up
yourself. Hope you're better.

But I *am* getting points in the news-
room—someone brought me coffee today
instead of saying get it yourself. I
could get used to this.

Think I'll be spoiled?

E-mail from: Ruby
To: Ed
Subject: *Spoilage*

Yeah, you're definitely spoilable. Are
they still standing in line to get your
coffee? I'm here to tell you that you
deserve it—the piece was awesome, and
you leave 'em panting for more from the
other two in the series.

Hope you're not hurting quite as much.
As for my pain—compared to a gunshot
wound, it's nothing—trust me. And it
felt a lot better after we talked on the
phone the other night.

Again, I loved your story. Maybe I'm
prejudiced, but this is Pulitzer material. Really.

E-mail from: Ed
To: Ruby
Subject:

You're prejudiced? Interesting. I'd
like to check that out.

E-mail from: Ruby
To: Ed
Subject:

When?

ACKNOWLEDGMENTS

To Suzy, David, Jon, Nancy, Emma, and Camille—family extraordinaire, and first readers, too.

To special people in my life who've given help and support during the research and writing of this book: Ruthe Winegarten, Suzanne Bloomfield, Lindsy Van Gelder, Pamela Brandt, Deena Mersky, Nancy Hendrickson, Nancy Bell, Judith Austin Mills, Karen Casey Fitzjerrell, Eileen Joyce, and Dena Garcia.

To Charlene Crilley, Suze Raff, and Kathi Stein, who helped make Ruby's Web site, *www.sharonkahn.com,* not only possible, but fun.

To Helen Rees of the Helen Rees Agency and Susanne Kirk, vice president and executive editor of Scribner, for their invaluable encouragement, and to Erik Wasson and Kim Hilario of Scribner, and Joan Mazmanian of the Helen Rees Agency.

To Carolyn Hessel, executive director of the Jewish Book Council, for all her help, and for the warmth and hospitality of the Jewish Book Fairs.

To the Hebrew Congregation of St. Thomas, for its *Short History of the Hebrew Congregation of St. Thomas,* other educational materials, and conversations.

Where it all began: special thanks to Barbara Peters of the Poisoned Pen Mystery Bookstore in Scottsdale, Arizona, who first suggested that Ruby visit the historic Jewish sites of the Caribbean.

ABOUT THE AUTHOR

Sharon Kahn has worked as an arbitrator, attorney, and freelance writer. She is a graduate of Vassar College and the University of Arizona Law School. The mother of three, and the former wife of a rabbi, she lives in Austin, Texas. *Fax Me a Bagel,* a Ruby, the Rabbi's Wife novel and her mystery debut, appeared in 1998. It was followed by *Never Nosh a Matzo Ball.*